"Lena, [...] **for me later? To catch up?"**

His stare was so dark, Lena felt herself slide into its endless depths. She fought the sensation with everything she had in her, stopping the headlong disaster at the very last moment.

She spoke slowly, distinctly. "I'm here today, Andres, because I had a job to do. As far as I'm concerned, that job is the only reason I'll be seeing you again. I certainly don't feel like going over old times."

"And if I disagree?"

Her pulse hammered, but Lena had trained herself well. She knew her expression was neutral. "Feel free to disagree all you want. I don't care one way or the other."

Before he could reply, she said, "The stairs are going to be our most open point. Stay as close to me as possible and keep your head down. When we hit the ground, we'll walk directly to the car. If anything happens, fall down. Understand?"

At her imperious tone, his own voice sharpened. "Lena, I know what to do. I've done this be—"

"Good. Then do it right, and we'll all come out alive."

They'd barely reached the bottom of the stairs when the first bullet slammed into the car.

Dear Reader,

The Commander holds a special place in my heart because
it tells the story of a very strong, very independent woman,
Lena McKinney. As the leader of Florida's Emerald Coast SWAT
team, Lena faces death daily. She fights crime and keeps victims
safe, leading fifteen men into dangerous operations around the
clock. But Lena isn't unique. Every woman reading this book
knows someone like Lena.

She could be your mother, she could be your boss, she could
be your next-door neighbor or your very best friend. Whoever she
is, she's someone you can depend on to be there when you need
her. She's someone who will listen to you complain and laugh at
your silly jokes. She's someone who will hold you when you cry
and comfort you when you're sad.

She's your inspiration.

I grew up in a family of strong women, the first of whom was
my grandmother. She raised five children by herself, cleaning
churches to put food on the table. Then there's my mom. A
survivor of cancer, she's the most incredible woman I know.
Sharp as they come, she can still run rings around everyone else
in the family. My sister's no slouch, either. She teaches elementary
school and has put two girls through college on her own. They will
be the next generation of formidable women.

A powerful woman deserves an exceptional man. He has to be her
equal in all ways, but he can't be threatened by her strength. He
has to appreciate it, to nurture it, to understand it. Fortunately for
Lena—and for the women in my family—men like that do exist.

While reading The Commander, I hope you come to appreciate
the strengths of all the characters, male and female. Most of all,
however, I hope you realize how many people like the ones I've
described—strong, special and powerful—there are in this world.
Chances are you're one of them!

Sincerely,

Kay David

The Commander
Kay David

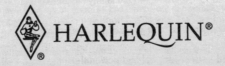

HARLEQUIN®

TORONTO • NEW YORK • LONDON
AMSTERDAM • PARIS • SYDNEY • HAMBURG
STOCKHOLM • ATHENS • TOKYO • MILAN • MADRID
PRAGUE • WARSAW • BUDAPEST • AUCKLAND

ISBN 0-373-70972-2

THE COMMANDER

This edition published by arrangement with Harlequin Books S.A.

® and TM are trademarks of the publisher. Trademarks indicated with ® are registered in the United States Patent and Trademark Office, the Canadian Trade Marks Office and in other countries.

Visit us at www.eHarlequin.com

Printed in U.S.A.

No author ever writes in a vacuum.
I always turn to many experts for help,
too many, in fact, to list here. Heartfelt thanks to everyone,
but the following three need special mention.

To Patricia Brown for generously sharing her medical
expertise regarding gunshot wounds. Thanks for the help,
but most of all, thanks for being such a great friend.

To Dr. Ron Grabowski for helping me with my anatomy
questions. You're a rare breed—someone who cares
and cares deeply. Thank you for everything.

To Caimee Schoenbaechler, one of my three beautiful,
intelligent nieces, for editing my Spanish. I wish I'd had you
with me in Argentina. People would have understood me
a heck of a lot better had you been my interpreter!

PROLOGUE

Somewhere off the coast of Cuba

THERE WAS no moon, thank God.

Andres Casimiro stared into the endless black of the water and counted the only blessing he had. If there'd been light, he'd be a dead man by now.

Easing the throttle of the boat, he slowed the vessel and cut the engine. The gentle sound of slapping waves replaced the throb of the motor, and he took a breath of something that felt like relief. No moonlight, no noise...he might have a chance.

In the still, hot quiet, he looked down at the chart on the table beside the wheel and checked his location again. His gaze traveled past the spot that marked his current position, and he drew a mental line from his home now—Miami—to the place he'd grown up—Havana: 198 nautical miles from one to the other. It should have been much farther, he thought. They were worlds apart. He shook his head to dislodge the thought. All he had to do right now was wait. Wait and *not* think.

Andres had never been a patient man, but in this instance, the waiting would be easier than the thinking anyway. He *had* to make his mind as empty as the sea beneath him to get through this. If he couldn't, the next few hours would be his last.

The minutes ticked by slowly. After a while, he lowered his arm to hide the light and pressed his watch to read the dial—1:00 a.m. Despite his best efforts to the contrary, a surge of disappointment— so strong it felt more like grief—washed over him. He and Lena would have been in Cancun by now, the wedding ceremony long behind them, the I do's said and sealed with a kiss. They would be settling into the villa on the beach. He'd reserved the last one on the Point, where no one ever came. He'd wanted the privacy, the intimacy of it. When he'd told Lena about the special house, she'd smiled in that secret way of hers and said one word. "Perfect."

He wondered what one word she had for him right now. It wasn't *perfect,* he was sure.

A tiny beam broke the darkness, unexpectedly radiant against the inky night before it winked out. Andres's heart bucked as if someone had punched him, and he fumbled the flashlight he'd been holding, dropping it to the deck. With a curse, he fell to his knees and patted the wooden planks. His fingers found the flashlight and he jumped up and flicked it once, then again. He thought he heard a splash, but he wasn't sure.

He started the countdown in his mind. They'd agreed on every thirty seconds. *One thousand one,* he began silently, *one thousand two...*

The numbers echoed in his mind, each digit accompanied by the same mantra. *Forgive me, Lena. I didn't have a choice.... Forgive me....*

He'd been completely unprepared for the phone call he'd gotten early that morning. Mateo's voice, coming over the tinny line, was the last one Andres had expected to hear only a few hours before his wedding. His best friend, Mateo Aznar had helped the eighteen-year-old Andres escape Cuba twenty-four years before and had served since as the sole source of information Andres had on the island. A former cop but now working for the Justice Department, Andres passed the intelligence on, most of it centering on one organization—the Red Tide. A drug cartel that purported to be freedom fighters, they had no good intentions.

"You've got to come," Mateo had gasped. "They've found out about everything. The radio, the lines, everything. If you can't get me out, they'll kill me."

Andres's breath had stopped. "But how did they—?"

"I have my suspicions."

"The same as mine?"

They hadn't wanted to say the name—in Cuba, there were ears everywhere. Andres wasn't sure Destin was any better.

"Sí," Mateo had replied. "I'm certain it's him."

"Do you have any proof?"

"I've got records of the payments. I think it's good enough together with what you know of his 'friends.'"

They'd gone on to what was needed, talking in a code they'd already developed. Within hours, Andres had been on a plane to Miami, then at the dock, renting the boat. He loved Lena desperately and the decision had torn him apart. But it was the only one he could make. When this was all over, he'd go back to her. He'd tell her what he could and pray she'd understand. Deep down, he knew she wouldn't, but to get through the night, he had to believe in the lie.

One thousand twenty-nine, one thousand thirty... Holding the flashlight above his head, Andres switched it on once more. His eyes searched the water. He'd anchored well offshore, but Mateo should have been visible by now. A movement to the right caught Andres's eye. Was it him? His palms pressing into the railing, Andres peered over the side of the boat.

If he hadn't been so focused, he might have seen them.

As it was, when the white-hot flash of the spotlight blinded him, Andres was astonished. The huge cutter loomed as suddenly as if the boat had been dropped from above. When his vision returned, shocked and in a panic, he shot his gaze back to the water. Twenty yards off the bow of his own vessel, he spotted Mateo, floundering in the waves. Before he could cry out, the larger boat angled between the two men.

"Put your hands up and prepare to be boarded. Drop any weapons *now!*" The warning was given in Spanish, through a bullhorn from the deck of the ship.

"*¿Comprende?*"

Instead of answering, Andres screamed into the night. "Hurry, Mateo, hurry! You can make it! Swim faster! I'll come get you!"

The water was choppy and rough, but Andres's and Mateo's eyes connected over the waves. In that instant, that split second, Andres knew he'd done the right thing. Leaving Lena at the altar, giving up the only woman he'd ever loved... How could he have lived with himself otherwise? He revved the engine then maneuvered the tiny boat around the cutter and headed toward his friend.

He reached Mateo just as an onslaught of bullets peppered the water. A searing pain streaked down Andres's arm as he took a direct hit, but the wound was nothing compared to the agony he felt as Mateo screamed and began to flail about in the now crimson waves.

"Goddammit, no! No!" Andres gunned the boat and cut past the spot, turning the craft as tightly as he dared to fly back once more. He searched the waves with desperate eyes, placing himself between the huge ship and where Mateo had been, but there was nothing to see.

Mateo was gone.

Andres screamed a useless curse and wasted a few more dangerous moments searching the water. With no other choice, he spun the boat around and disappeared into the darkness. Gunfire followed his wake, but it couldn't reach him. His craft was fast and small, and the cutter didn't have a chance.

He made it to Miami a few hours later. He'd sacrificed love for loyalty, a wife for a friend.

Now he had neither. It'd take him a lifetime to forget.

And forever to forgive.

CHAPTER ONE

Destin, Florida
Two years later

LENA MCKINNEY stepped onto the red-carpeted aisle of the flower-filled church, the solemn strains of the ''Wedding March'' drifting above the crowded pews.

All the guests were watching her and she knew what they were thinking—little Lena McKinney was *finally* getting married…after all this time! Her tomboy years were behind her, and now she was a woman. From beneath her lacy veil she smiled with silent satisfaction, then all at once, the realization hit her.

Other than the veil, she wore nothing. She was completely naked.

A wave of humiliation swamped her as she dropped her bouquet and tried to cover herself. Her actions were pointless, though. Everyone had already seen. Everyone already knew.

With a startled exclamation, Lena woke up and pushed herself out of the tangled sheets of her bed.

She glanced at the clock on the nightstand, her heart still pounding from the dream—5:00 a.m. What in the hell was she doing? She had to get up in another hour, and now she'd never go back to sleep. She never did after the dream.

She collapsed against her pillows, muttering a curse then immediately chastising herself. Her poor mother was probably turning over in her grave. That's what came from eating, breathing and drinking your work, Lena thought guiltily. She was starting to sound like the testosterone-charged cops she worked with 24/7.

No excuse, her mother's ghost said with a hopeless sigh. You're *supposed* to be a lady, try acting like one for a change.

Lena stared at the stained ceiling above her bed. At least her mother hadn't been alive to see the Disaster, which was how Lena always thought of the aborted wedding.

The beautiful sanctuary, the silken gown, the wonderful music…every detail coordinated down to her bouquet of white freesias and apricot roses. They'd waited for as long as they could, her father holding her hand in the tiny room off the narthex, then they'd sent out Bering, the eldest of her four brothers. He'd explained as much as possible, and the guests had gone home. Lena had been worried, then incredulous, both emotions finally exploding into a bitter anger the next day when Andres had shown up and given her his lame excuses.

Get a grip, she told herself furiously. It was past

history. Dead and gone. Andres had moved on and
so had she. Stationed in Miami, he was climbing
the ladder at the Justice Department, going up so
fast he was nothing but a blur. She hadn't been
standing still, either. In charge of the Emerald
Coast SWAT team, Lena held a position of authority and power, too. Two cells of topflight officers worked under her command.

Moaning with disgust over the dream and at herself for having it, Lena sat up and put her feet on
the floor. A front had blown in last night and the
stained concrete was cold and hard, the icy feeling
instantly traveling up her legs. The scene outside
the uncovered windows added to the chill, a gray
and stormy Floridian sea churning on the beach
only a hundred yards away. Above the waves, the
October sky looked just as forbidding. Dark, heavy
clouds hovered over the horizon, their swirling
depths promising rain later.

One of the panes of glass rattled loudly, and
propelled by the sound, Lena turned to go to the
kitchen. The pipes sang, the shingles leaked, and
half the time the heater refused to work. She didn't
care. She had memories of her mother here, and of
good summers, laughing and chasing her brothers
over the dunes. Her father had tried to buy her a
condo last summer in the new high-rise going up
off Inlet Beach. The units were "only" three hundred thousand, he'd said. A bargain at preconstruc-
tion rates. She'd turned him down, and he'd gotten
angry, not understanding.

In the kitchen, she flipped on the television set, reaching for the door of the refrigerator at the same time. Bleary-eyed, she grabbed the last diet cola and a boiled egg left over from a few days before. The breakfast of champions. Her planned stop at the grocery store yesterday had been put on hold, as a lot of her plans were, when the team had gotten a late-afternoon call-out. The situation had dragged on forever, and they hadn't cleaned up the mess until after two that morning. But that's what SWAT team work was like. You stayed until the end, no matter how long it took to come.

No one had been hurt, though. That was always her goal: everyone gets out alive.

She popped open the cold drink, then took a long swallow before beginning to peel the egg, dropping the bits of shell into the sink. "Everyone gets out alive," she repeated out loud. "Hostages, victims...even jilted brides."

The ringing phone startled her and Lena fumbled with the egg. She caught it right before it slid into the disposal, then grabbed the receiver. "McKinney here."

Sarah Greenberg's soft voice sounded, and Lena relaxed the muscles she'd tightened automatically on hearing the phone. Sarah was the SWAT team's information officer, and her calls didn't usually signify an emergency. "Sarah! You're calling awfully early. What's up? Everything okay?"

"We're fine," the young woman answered.

Lena sipped her cola. "Did Beck tell you about

last night?'' A former negotiator, Beck Winters had left the SWAT team a while back but Lena had promised him a desk job and he'd returned.

Before Sarah could answer, Lena launched into an explanation. ''Panama City Beach had a warrant they were trying to serve. It went downhill fast, but—'' She realized suddenly that Sarah had gone silent. Usually the young cop had plenty to contribute but for some reason, she hadn't said a word. Lena frowned. ''Sarah?''

A pause—this one lasting long enough to make Lena really nervous—then Sarah spoke. ''We got a fax this morning ordering a special dignitary detail for next week. I thought you might want to know about it right away so you could... um...prepare for it.''

''I'll be in the office in an hour,'' Lena said slowly. ''It couldn't wait until then?''

''I thought you might want to know about this one before you got here...so you wouldn't be surprised.''

Lena waited a minute, but Sarah said nothing more and finally Lena spoke again, this time somewhat impatiently. ''Well, are you going to tell me or do I have to guess?''

''It's for the guy from Justice in Miami.'' Sarah sounded almost shaky. ''You know, the one they're sending to open the new office? There've been death threats called in. They think an attempt might be made on his life.''

She should have known, Lena told herself later.

She should have seen it coming. But it was only after Sarah said "Miami" that Lena's mind kicked into gear. "No...oh, no... Shit..."

"I'm sorry, Lena. But it's Andres Casimiro. He's coming to Destin and he needs protection."

"Is THIS THE FULL REPORT?" Andres raised his gaze to Carmen San Vicente, his assistant. They were in the director's private jet, fifteen thousand feet above the Florida Panhandle. Andres hadn't taken the time to look out the window and see the turquoise waters beneath him, but he'd buzzed the captain a moment before and asked for the ETA. The man had said ten minutes and Andres had felt his gut respond accordingly. Now he was glaring at Carmen and she had no idea she wasn't responsible for his expression. He was thinking of the same thing he'd been thinking of for the past week—every day, every hour, every minute—since he'd known he was coming back to Destin.

Lena.

Carmen answered, but Andres's mind had already gone elsewhere. He hadn't spoken to Lena since the night he'd returned to Destin following Mateo's death. The meeting had been disastrous, of course. He'd told her what he could—that a special mission had come up, that he'd had no choice but to miss their wedding.

She'd stared him in the eye and said just what he'd expected, her voice calm and controlled. "I'm a cop, Andres. I would have understood if you'd told me.''

With his heart cracking in two, he'd met her accusing stare. It had held equal shares of pain and anger, and he'd felt both just as deeply. ''I couldn't tell you, Lena. Not this time.''

She'd looked as if she wanted to believe him, but a moment later she'd closed her expression. ''Then we have nothing more to discuss.'' Pulling off the diamond he'd given her, she'd handed him the ring and turned away. ''Please leave.''

He'd done what she asked because he hadn't had another choice. And he still didn't. To begin with, she would never believe him, and if she did accept his suspicions—by some miracle—it would almost be worse. The news would completely destroy her.

Lena's father had arranged Mateo Aznar's death. He'd wanted to kill Andres, as well.

Andres had had his suspicions before the wedding, but for Lena's sake, he'd kept them to himself. He'd waited and watched, collected the tiny scraps of evidence he could, the main one being a local drug dealer named Pablo Escada, who had kept Phillip McKinney's law office on retainer. The Panamanian immigrant was in the Union Correctional Institution for the moment, but he hadn't shut down his business. Andres couldn't prove the connection but he knew—he *knew*—Escada was hooked up with the Red Tide. He had to be. The organization funneled all the drugs that came through the area.

And Phillip was connected to Escada.

For months after the murder, Andres had devoted every minute of his time trying to document Phillip's involvement, but he'd ended up with nothing. He'd been unable to find a shred of data, an iota of validation, to link the wily old attorney with the terrorists.

After a while, Andres had to let it go and accept what appeared to be the truth: things had gone terribly wrong that night and the Red Tide had acted on their own. Mateo had been wrong about the money coming from Phillip's office.

"I brought everything that was in the folder." Carmen's voice held an anxious flutter. "Are you missing something?"

Andres finally heard her apologetic tone. He shook his head. "I'm sorry. I didn't mean to bark at you. I'm a little preoccupied—"

"It's okay," she answered in an accommodating way. "I understand. Really, I do. It's impossible to get anything done when you have to travel all the time." She reached up and tucked a strand of dark hair behind one ear then her eyes warmed hopefully as Andres's gaze met hers. "Would you like to work this evening? I could come to your hotel room after dinner tonight and we could finish this then."

"No," he said, shaking his head. "We'll cover the final details right before the meeting in the morning. It's not necessary to take you away from your kids *and* make you work overtime, too."

Andres watched her hide her disappointment by turning away to fuss with some files in her hands. With her shining hair and olive skin, she had the kind of beauty for which Miami's women were famous. Years before, she'd befriended his aunt Isabel, and the older woman, more of a mother to him than his own had been, had convinced him to hire Carmen when she'd needed a job. She was smart and ambitious, a single mom with two children she was putting through private school.

She'd finally gotten him into bed the month before.

He'd known the minute it started, he was making a big mistake. He'd tried to tell her, to back away and bow out gracefully, but she'd put her fingers across his mouth and stopped him from saying more. When her lips had left his and gone lower, he'd said nothing else, allowing her hot eyes and slow touch to comfort him. But he should never have given in. It'd been unfair to her.

Carmen started toward the front of the plane, then stopped at the bulkhead and turned, as though just remembering something. "Did you get your vest?"

He stared at her blankly. "My vest?"

"The director left a bulletproof vest for you to wear when you get off the plane. He told me he'd have my head if you weren't wearing it when you arrived."

Andres dismissed her words with a wave of his hand. It was a very Latin gesture; as a child, he'd seen his Cuban father make the same one a thousand times.

"I *promised* him," she said.

"You shouldn't have. They're hot and heavy and totally useless. I never wore one when I was a cop and I'm not going to start now." He went back to the files spread before him.

"And did the Red Tide have money on your head while you were a cop?"

"Drop it, Carmen. I don't have the time or the patience."

Ignoring him, she came back down the aisle and rested on the arm of the seat opposite his. "*Por favor*, Andres, those guys are terrorists. They're bad—"

"They're leftover Communists and rejects from the islands who sell drugs. Don't be confused about this, Carmen." He narrowed his gaze. "They're criminals and nothing more. If I let scum like that scare me, then I don't deserve to be in this job."

"They've threatened to kill you."

"So what? They've done the same before and nothing has happened. We've ordered security at the airport. Let the Emerald Coast SWAT team handle this."

He turned his eyes out the window of the plane. Destin was almost in view. What would Lena say to him? How would she react after all this time?

Carmen started to argue more, but the captain's

voice came over the intercom. "Two minutes to landing, folks. Everyone buckle up."

"I'll get the vest for you right now." She tried one last time. "You can slip it on before we land—"

"No." He slammed his files shut and pulled on his seat belt. "No one's going to be shooting at anybody. Not the Red Tide. Not anybody. Not today."

Carmen shook her head then sat down abruptly in the seat in front of him, the sound of her own seat belt an angry click as she buckled herself in.

But Andres hardly noticed. Once again, he wasn't thinking about his assistant or the Red Tide or even the man he'd suspected all those years ago of backing them. His thoughts were centered on the only thing he really cared about in Destin.

Lena McKinney.

The woman he'd never stopped loving.

LENA STOOD beneath the overhang of Terminal A, her eyes scanning the buildings around her as the breeze tugged at her hair and pulled on her jacket. The sky was so blue, it almost glowed. Strong winds straight from the Gulf had blown away last week's storm clouds and now it was clear, the sunshine warming the temperature to a balmy seventy degrees, the quick change typical for Destin's weather. A salty tang hung over the blackened tarmac, as well. The airport was blocks from the beach, but the sea was always close in Destin.

Even if it wasn't in sight, you could either hear it or smell it.

Her earphone crackled suddenly and Lena put her fingers against the small black piece of plastic all the team members wore in order to communicate with each other. The words sounded faintly in her ear. Andres's plane would be landing within minutes.

She lifted her gaze to the cloudless expanse. The aircraft was not yet in sight, but she could feel its nearness deep inside her. Ever since Sarah had given her the news, Lena had hovered between craziness and calm acceptance. One minute she'd tell herself she could handle Andres's appearance. He no longer meant anything to her, anything at all. The next minute lunacy would take over and she'd start to recall everything about him—his black eyes, his heavy-lidded looks, the Latin sighs.

Standing on the asphalt, she told herself there was only one way this meeting would go. He'd arrive, she'd say a cool hello, then she'd concentrate on her job and nothing else. Keeping him safe was all she had to worry about and nothing could interfere with that goal.

Everyone gets out alive.

To maintain her calmness, she focused on her preparations. The airport was tiny and that made things simple. Their primary concern would be the deplaning. Passengers didn't always go through jetways here; sometimes after the aircraft landed, they walked down exterior stairways. He'd be the most vulnerable right then. That was why she would go out and meet him personally. Her chest went tight at the thought, but she took a deep breath and concentrated on the details.

She'd put Ryan Lukas, their main sniper, on the center roof and his counterpart from the other team, Chase Mitchell, on the rear building. Peter Douglas and John Fletcher, the two rear entry men from Team Beta were manning security at the entrances inside and out. Cal Hamilton and Jason Field, the rear guys from Alpha were providing undercover surveillance inside the waiting lounges. She'd ordered dogs and handlers into the parking garage as a final extra precaution. The remaining team members she'd scattered about the airport, leaving only a skeleton crew in town under the control of her second in command, Bradley Thompson. Maybe she'd gone overboard, but she didn't want to examine that thought too closely, so she told herself if nothing else, it was good training for the day when someone really important might show up.

The low, thrumming sound of a jet interrupted the expectant silence. When Lena spotted its blue-and-white logo, she reached up and adjusted her headset to bring the microphone closer to her mouth. ''Head's up, everyone. Package approaching.''

Her voice was level and constant. *It's just another job,* she told herself. Another situation, another call-out, nothing more. Andres was coming to meet with the head of the new D.E.A. branch office that was opening in Destin. According to Sarah, he'd be in and out in one day. She'd see him for a total of ten minutes, coming and going, and that was it.

Everyone gets out alive.

The plane came into view and a few seconds later, the wheels touched down, their screaming protest louder than Lena was accustomed to from inside the terminal. In a matter of minutes, the jet reached the end of the blackened asphalt, then turned slowly and began to taxi toward her. Lena's gaze went over the area one more time, checking and rechecking. Everyone on the field had gone through security, but a sudden edginess brushed against her. She didn't believe in omens but all at once her instincts were screaming too loud to ignore. She concentrated a moment more, then her gaze homed in on the porthole in the aft section of the arriving plane, pinpointing the source of her discomfort. Her unease was coming from *inside* the aircraft, not out.

A face stared at her through the thick glass of the window. She caught only an impression—dark hair and a black suit—but it was enough. She knew it was Andres. The engines whined loudly and the plane ended up alongside the waiting stairway. A moment later, the noise from the turbines died, leaving only silence.

Lena walked into the bright sunshine and headed for the stairs.

CHAPTER TWO

ANDRES ROSE from his seat, nervous energy propelling him into the aisle before the jet had even stopped moving. Pacing the tiny walkway, he waited for the flight attendant to open the door, willing the man to hurry up, but without obvious results. A rush of humid air and sunshine flooded the cabin as the uniformed steward finally drew the door back.

He told himself he was prepared.

But he wasn't.

Lena stepped inside and Andres's heart stopped. He could actually feel it thump once then quit. A moment later, it started again, but for a second, he hadn't been sure it would.

Her whiplike body filled the black SWAT uniform with unmistakable familiarity. She'd never had a voluptuous figure, but what she did have was perfect. She was fit and trim without an ounce of extra anything. Her brown hair, still shiny and smooth, was tinged with streaks of blond and cut shorter than he remembered. Her gray eyes weren't as stormy as they'd been the last time he'd seen her, but there was something in her gaze that stabbed him, the pain unexpectedly pointed and physical.

"Andres." She said his name with aloofness. "Welcome to Destin."

"Thank you, Lena. It's good to see you—"

She didn't let him finish, her brisk response impersonal and distant. "We need to do this fast, Andres. The longer we take, the more opportunity for trouble there is." Tilting her head, she indicated the stairs behind her. "I'll go down first. You follow me. Scott will get your back. Everyone else comes off after you're clear."

He knew it was foolish but Andres found himself wanting something else from her, something...more. The realization bothered him, but he put it aside and looked at the man behind her. He was young but had the hard air of a seasoned cop. Wearing the same uniform as Lena, black and tight, he acknowledged Andres with a quick bob of his head as Lena spoke again, her voice even more clipped and cold.

"You've got on the vest?"

"No," he said brusquely. "The vest is not necessary."

"We're not deplaning until you have it on."

"You're wasting my time."

"No," she answered in a no-nonsense way. "You're wasting it yourself." Her eyes flicked over his shoulder and she spoke to Carmen, figuring out her status instantly. "Do you know where his Kevlar vest is?" Carmen apparently nodded, and Lena continued. "Go get it, please."

Her manner brought forth another flash of irritation. She always did it by the book, no matter what. He glanced down at his watch then looked back up at her. "I have to be downtown in fifteen minutes."

Carmen appeared at Lena's side and handed her a small black bag. Without even looking at it, Lena handed the pack over to him. "Then put this on, and we'll leave."

He glared at her and she glared back, but a moment later, he snatched the bag from her hands and pulled out the black sleeveless garment. His eyes remained on her face as he ripped off his tie and began to unbutton his jacket. "This is ridiculous." When he was upset a trace of Spanish inflection always came into his voice. He heard it now. "You've made the area safe, no? Why should I do this?"

"Because I'm not perfect," she told him calmly. "And neither are the men who work for me. We've swept the terminal and have people in place, but you never know. Someone could have slipped through."

He pulled off his black silk coat and shrugged into the Kevlar, the fabric stiff against his white, starched shirt. In the closeness of the cabin, he could smell her soap…or was he imagining it?

"I'm trusting you to have done your job right," he snapped. "You should be flattered, not giving me a hard time."

Her steady eyes revealed nothing in response to his words, but a vibration of energy came off her body, a low, silent humming that only Andres could have caught. His fingers stilled on the fasteners of the vest as she spoke.

"My job will be done when you're off this plane and still alive." A heartbeat passed as her gray eyes locked on his. "Trust has nothing to do with it."

ANDRES GATHERED his briefcase and jacket while Lena stood at the door of the plane and surveyed the runway area one more time. Her eyes went slowly over the buildings in front of her, but in fact, she wasn't really seeing them. The image coming to her instead was that of Andres and his hands. When she thought of him, she always thought of those hands. Other women might have noticed his trim stomach or the width of his shoulders or even his eyes as they'd stared at her, but not Lena. She'd watched his fingers move over the buttons of his blazer. They were long, his knuckles slim and well-formed, his wrists broad and strong-looking.

She'd noticed the rest of him, too, though. Above the collar of his pristine white shirt, the café-au-lait tone of his skin, that sweet, smooth color she'd always loved, was darker than before, the contrast of the material against his face and neck sensual and appealing. When he was under a lot of stress, he spent as much time as he could outdoors, playing baseball usually.

Beneath all the polish, though, he acted just as he always had—like a banked fire poised on the verge of explosion. She'd responded as she'd known she would, too, with the same mix of fascination and dread and anger he always created inside her. Nothing she could say to herself would make her heart stop crashing inside her chest. How could she do what she was supposed to do? How could she concentrate?

All she could think about was the last time they'd been together, when he'd shown up after the canceled wedding and told her about the special operation he'd had to run. She'd been a cop all her adult life and a good one; even though his distrust had hurt, she had understood the need for secrecy, the reticence to talk. But she was a woman, too. He'd broken her heart and destroyed her self-confidence. She could never forgive him for that.

As she always did when her thinking got too heavy, she turned to action, forcing herself to focus as she pulled her microphone closer. "L1 calling team leader. Package secure."

"Gotcha, L1. We're clear. Wait for final check then proceed."

They transmitted on closed channels, but when doing protections Lena insisted on maintaining as much security as possible. With a precise, calm voice, she checked on each of the team members, using the code they'd already agreed on. Everyone was in place and ready to move. When Ryan, the sniper, issued a final clear from his vantage point, they'd go. She looked over her shoulder, past Scott to where Andres stood.

He was giving some last-minute instructions to the woman who'd brought Lena his vest. His secretary, his assistant, his lover? Lena wasn't sure of her position, but she'd immediately known how the woman felt about Andres. Her adoration of him was obvious. It meant nothing to Lena, of course, yet she couldn't help but notice. When they'd been together, he'd continually attracted women. They couldn't seem to resist him.

Passing Scott, Andres moved to the front of the cabin and took up his position directly behind her. He'd donned his jacket again and the bulky vest beneath made his chest look vast. As he juggled his briefcase to his other hand, he bumped into her shoulder. *"Lo siento,"* he murmured. *I'm sorry....*

The Spanish was unexpected and somehow too intimate. She looked directly at him then, and in the closeness, all her senses, the ones she'd been trying to tamp down since she'd walked into the plane and into his presence, heightened, as if someone had turned up a volume knob until the sound was out of range. She could smell his aftershave, a scent she didn't recognize, thank God, and even see the tiny flecks of gold imbedded in the iris of his right eye. She had on a SWAT jacket and vest as well, but the brush of his arm burned through the fabric like a lighted torch.

She couldn't physically step away; she was trapped between him and the door, but she pulled into herself and shuttered her expression, turning her face away from him.

Her coldness didn't stop him. Impulsively, it appeared, he reached out and drew a line down the side of her cheek. His touch was as smooth and sensual as ever and it left a trail of stunning memories behind. "Lena..." He gave her name the Spanish inflection. "Will you have some time for me later? To catch up?"

His stare was so black, Lena felt herself slide into its endless depths. She fought the sensation with everything she had in her, stopping the headlong disaster only at the very last moment. She spoke slowly, distinctly. "I'm here today because I have a job to do. And as far as I'm concerned, that job is the only reason I'll be seeing you again. I have nothing else to say to you and I certainly don't feel like going over old times."

"And if I disagree?"

Her pulse jackhammered, but Lena had trained herself well. She knew her expression was neutral.

"Feel free to disagree all you want. I don't really care one way or the other."

His eyes danced over her face, searching it for something, and she felt the plunge begin again. Before his inexorable pull could drag her any deeper, her radio sounded, Ryan's voice in her ear. "This is G1. Area clear. L1 proceed."

She acknowledged the call, then spoke to Andres, heading off whatever his reply might have been.

"The stairs are going to be our most open point. Stay as close to me as possible and keep your head down. Don't look around. Just watch my feet and go where I go. Scott will be at your back. When we hit the ground, we'll walk directly to the car. If anything happens, fall down. Understand?"

At her imperious tone, his own voice sharpened. "For God's sake, Lena, I know what to do. I've done this before—"

"Good," she broke in. "Then do it right, and we'll all come out alive."

He started to reply, but at the last minute he snapped his mouth shut and jerked his head toward the stairs in an impatient let's-go motion. Lena caught Scott's eye, spoke into her headset then started down the stairs.

As ANDRES FOLLOWED Lena down the steps, he told himself to calm down, to act as if he didn't care. It was an impossible order, though.

He'd never be able to do that, not as far as she was concerned.

When she'd made that crack about trust, Lena had been putting him on notice. There was no trust between them—not now. She would do her job but there would be no other contact. She wanted nothing to do with him. Nothing at all.

Forcing himself to ignore his response, he discarded Lena's instructions and looked around the tarmac, his stare quick and jumpy as it traveled over the jetway and to the buildings beyond. He saw nothing unusual.

To their right a mechanic in a set of blue overalls worked under the hood of a small Cessna, his tools laid out in a precise line at his feet. To his left, a man in sunglasses and a cap sat behind the wheel of a small motorized cart filled with luggage. In between them was the terminal, and through a wall of windows, Andres could see a group of passengers mingling and talking. Well-dressed and well-heeled, they matched the expensive designer suitcases on the wagon. They were probably waiting for one of the private jets that made up the majority of planes coming in and out of the airport.

By the time he finished his scan, they were at the foot of the stairs, and Andres took a deep breath, an unconscious sweep of relief hitting him hard. For the first time, he noticed the weather; the sunshine was almost blinding, the air warmer and softer than it usually was this time of year. Along the walkway, a row of sago palms swayed in the brisk breeze, their green fronds gleaming in the light.

A second later they reached a nearby SUV. The unmarked Suburban, painted black with darkly tinted windows, was so obviously a government truck it could have had the department's seal on the side. The back doors swung wide, and Zack Potter stepped out. Potter would be running the Destin office Andres was here to officially open. A former D.C. policeman, the handsome man looked more like a bodybuilder than a federal official. They'd been friends a long time and Andres respected him greatly. Except for Andres himself, no one could run the office any better. With Zack Potter in charge, the Red Tides's pipeline of drugs from Mexico to New York was about to hit a major roadblock.

Potter crossed the space between them and held out his hand, a wide grin splitting his face. "Casimiro! 'Bout time you got here." He nodded toward the jet. "Nice ride, too!"

"Let's save the greetings for later, gentlemen." Lena glanced in Potter's direction, then spoke quickly, her eyes studying the area around them as she motioned Scott to the other side of the car. "I need to get Mr. Casimiro inside, please...."

"Of course, of course!" Potter smiled again then stepped aside to let Andres pass. Lena stood at the door of the truck waiting for him.

He reached her side, threw his briefcase onto the seat, then turned to look at her. Just as in the plane, they were inches apart, her slim form backed up against the open car door, his body poised to get inside. Her gaze was serene and composed, the stone color of her eyes even more intense now that they were outside in the sunshine. It was crazy, but he had to try—and he wasn't even sure for what— one more time.

"Lena...*querida*..."

Again the Spanish. Lena couldn't believe it, but something curled inside her, a warm yearning for a time that was far behind them. The depth of pain that accompanied the craving surprised her, but she stiffened against it. She wasn't his sweetheart and hadn't been for a long time. How dare he use that word and that tone of voice? How was she supposed to deal with that?

Before she could form her angry reply, she caught an unexpected movement in her peripheral vision, a sudden motion that made her snap to, almost as if waking up from a dream. She glanced toward the area, already cursing herself for letting down her guard. Her profanity had barely cleared the air when the first bullet slammed into the Suburban.

A moment later, the second one came.

Beside them, Zack Potter collapsed onto the asphalt, his scream dying as the bullet ripped into his neck. Lena stared at his still-jerking body, then she yanked her head up and cried into her headset for backup. As she spoke, she whirled and Andres's shocked eyes met hers. Grabbing his arms instinctively, she did what she was trained to do—she pushed him straight into the truck.

But he resisted her, and for one single second, they held on to each other, each trying their best to protect the other one first. Lena won—not by strength—but by doing the only thing she could. She went limp. Caught off guard by her action, Andres hesitated and that was all she needed. With a violent shove, she forced him down, then turned, thrusting herself in front of him.

The final shot was a direct hit. Lena crumpled without a word.

CHAPTER THREE

ANDRES REACTED instantly, old habits taking over as adrenaline kicked in. He grabbed Lena by the collar of her jacket and yanked her to him. Still trying to draw her weapon, she fought him futilely. "No," she gasped. "You go! Get in the car and leave!"

"Not without you!" They wasted a few more precious moments, then too weak to do anything else, she gave in to Andres and allowed him to pull her into the truck. Before he tumbled inside the vehicle with her, Andres sent a quick glance in Zack Potter's direction. The time to help his friend had passed. "Get us out of here," he roared to the driver. "Now! Let's go!"

The man needed no urging. The black SUV sprang forward, the tires squealing as he drove it down the sidewalk and straight toward a set of double gates. Only when she spoke again did Andres realize Lena had never released her grip of his arm. She pulled at him weakly, her voice fading but still urgent. "Stay down. We don't know where the shots came from."

Andres turned, but it was too late for her to hear his reply. Her eyes rolled back and she fainted without a sound. Her limp body started to pitch off the seat, but he threw himself on top of her and stopped her fall at the very last minute. Bracing himself, he fought the violent rocking of the truck and prepared for the crash of the vehicle as it went through the metal frame of the gate.

When it didn't happen, he lifted his head and took a quick glance. A figure in black, one of Lena's men, had swung back the iron grilles. The driver deftly maneuvered through the narrow opening, then bumped the speeding vehicle over the grooved tracks to a grassy swell just at the left of the runway. With the tires screaming even louder than before, the Suburban hit the pavement outside the terminal then turned right on two wheels. Within seconds they were on the main road into town, two black and whites escorting them, one front, one rear.

In the back of his mind, Andres realized what he had just witnessed. Lena had planned for this. She'd had a man stationed at the exit and an escape route in place.

The man behind the wheel said something about alerting the hospital, then spoke into a headset. "Let them know we're bringing someone in," he said shakily. His voice thickened as he answered an obvious question. "No, it's not the package. It's Lieutenant McKinney. She's been hit."

Beneath Andres, Lena groaned. He slid to the floorboard of the vehicle to give her more room, then he took a good look at her injury for the first time. The bullet had managed to go beneath her vest. It didn't look good. His mouth went dry.

''Where's the first aid—''

Before he could finish, the driver thrust a white metal box over the front seat. ''There's bandages and tape inside,'' he said. ''We'll be at the hospital in five minutes.''

Andres ripped open the case and grabbed a roll of white gauze, but the material was woefully inadequate. It seemed as if blood was pouring from Lena. Yanking off his coat, he pressed it against the wound but the fabric was immediately soaked. He'd seen plenty of men shot, had even done the shooting himself more than once, but this was Lena, for God's sake. She groaned and a sick feeling rose up in his chest to block his breathing.

He slipped a hand beneath her head. She was going into shock, her skin pale and clammy, her body shaking on the leather cushions that were already slick with her blood. Her eyes fluttered open, and suddenly she looked smaller and more frail.

''Hang on, *querida,* hang on.'' His endearment slipped out naturally, just as it had earlier in the plane. ''We'll be at the hospital any minute. You can do it.''

She spoke with great difficulty. ''You...okay? Not hit?''

"Don't talk," he said automatically. "You'll lose more blood."

She ignored him completely. "Are you...okay?"

"*Sí, sí.* I am fine, now *por favor*—no more talking!"

She nodded weakly, her eyes closing once more, only to blink open again. "W-what about... Potter?"

"Don't worry about him. The others will take care of him. You just lie there and be quiet."

They bounced around a curve. She tried to bite back a cry but failed, her agony apparent. Helpless to do anything else, Andres screamed at the driver. "Take it easy up there, goddammit! You're hurting her!"

The man didn't respond; he simply added more gas, the black Suburban barreling down the highway, passing everything else in a blur.

"Andres..." She spoke his name softly, painfully.

He bent down, his heart suddenly plunging into a frightening abyss. She was fading right before his eyes, growing obviously weaker as he held on to her. "Lena! Stay with me, okay? Stay awake!"

She lifted a shaking hand and grabbed his shirt. Her fingers were red and sticky with her own blood, but the strength in her grip was shocking. She pulled him closer, her voice a fading rasp. "I should have done a better job...shoulda checked better.'' Her lips were dried and caked, the words thick but the meaning clear. ''I'm sorry, Andres, I'm so sorry....''

She was apologizing for saving his life? If there were *shoulds* they belonged to him, dammit! *He* should have been the one lying there bleeding, not Lena.

He leaned over her. ''Lena, please! You *did* do your job. Don't get *loco* on me, okay? *¿Me escuchas?* Do you hear me?''

She nodded faintly, then she went still in his arms and her head fell back.

ANDRES DIDN'T KNOW which was worse: holding Lena's unresponsive body or handing her over to the medics at the hospital. Either way he felt helpless and totally out of control.

Three nurses and two doctors were waiting as the SUV wheeled into the drive-through by the hospital's back door. They shoved him out of the way and disappeared with Lena down the hall. He caught up to the gurney just as they turned it into a room and slammed the door in his face. All he could do was listen as someone screamed for X rays STAT and another voice yelled out for a chest tube. He vented his frustration by cursing in Spanish and waving his arms but his actions were futile. No one would let him inside.

Leaning his head against the mint-colored wall, a storm of emotion broke over him. Panic, anger, fear, guilt—every feeling he'd ever experienced erupted all at once. It was a tide he couldn't stop, a flood he couldn't control. In a useless attempt to stem the sensations, he raised his hands to cover his face, but all he did was make it worse as his fingers came into focus.

The creases in his skin were painted red. Red with Lena's blood. His horrified gaze fell lower. His pants, his shirt, even his shoes were crimson. He was covered with her blood.

He stared a moment longer, then he closed his fingers, his knuckles shining under the bright lights of the corridor as a rush of guilty rage shook him. Lifting his arm in one fluid movement, he slammed his fist into the wall. A hole appeared as a rain of green plaster cascaded to the floor.

His whole side went numb, but his mind—and his heart—cracked open wide.

THE DOCTORS and the nurses were talking. Their voices were hurried, but distinct, each word a perfectly formed entity that Lena heard, then saw. They floated above her, just out of reach in little cartoon boxes, as did the masked faces of the people nearby. She wanted to tell them she felt fine but everyone seemed too rushed to listen to her mumbles. She closed her eyes slowly, the lids fluttering down. The next thing she knew, she was at the beach. Jeffrey, the youngest of all her brothers, was chasing her into the tide, splashing her and calling her a baby, telling her about the monsters that were just offshore, waiting to get her.

She looked out into the emerald waves and shivered. Monsters were out there, all right, but they weren't in the water. They were closer, closer than either of them had ever suspected. She shut her eyes and screamed, but no one heard her.

ANDRES HEARD Phillip McKinney long before he saw him, the man's unmistakable voice rolling down the hallway and bowling over everything in its path. Andres jumped to his feet and after a questioning glance, Carmen, at his side, stood as well. A moment later, Lena's father strode into the waiting room, his entourage following behind him as he plowed through the crowd of cops who'd begun to congregate after hearing the news.

Phillip had aged a bit, but not that much. His hair, always silver, was a little thinner and his step a little slower, yet his back was ramrod straight, his skin tanned and tight. The handmade suit, the polished shoes, the silk foulard tie, they hadn't changed at all. Expensive and flashy, they were essential to Phillip's presence.

At seventy, he was a still practicing attorney with personal injury lawsuits his speciality. His thriving partnership had given him the kind of wealth and power few men could ever achieve; he was well-known all over Florida and even in the nearby states.

Almost as an afterthought, Andres's brain registered the identities of the men surrounding Phillip. They were Lena's brothers, all older than her except for Jeffrey, the baby of the family. Bering, the eldest, waited anxiously just beside his father. On the other side of the old man was Richard, her second brother. Behind those two came Stephen, and finally, trailing, came Jeffrey.

As always, Jeff was a peripheral member of the group. Even though he worked at Phillip's law firm alongside his brothers, he was the black sheep of the family. Idealistic and sometimes naive to Andres's way of thinking, Jeff continually disavowed what he considered the other McKinneys's base materialism. He spent his vacations helping migrant workers and went his own way, a way that was usually the opposite of what Phillip McKinney wanted.

Which was exactly why Andres had liked Jeff and had called him to inform the family of the shooting. He couldn't stand the rest of them.

Shaking hands and greeting the officers, most of whom he seemed to know, Phillip McKinney was almost on top of Andres before he noticed him. He didn't have time to prepare himself, so instead a cascade of emotions, genuine and unedited, crossed his expression at once. First surprise then anger, and finally a wary edginess, all of which he hid as soon as he could behind a stony mask.

Andres stared back from behind his own facade.

He'd never known if the old man was aware of the investigation he'd conducted against him or not. Regardless, they'd hated each other from the very moment they'd met. Phillip had told Lena that Andres wasn't good enough for her, but the real truth was a lot more complicated. Phillip had had Lena to himself since her mother died and he didn't want to share her, with a husband or anyone else. It was power and control and love, all mixed together.

Phillip recovered fast. "How is she?" Silky smooth and deep, his voice was his trademark. It now held a tinge of something Andres had never heard before. Fear? Concern? Love?

"Lena's in surgery," Andres answered. "The bullet entered her body just beneath her left breast. They reinflated her lung in ER, then took her into the operating room."

Phillip sagged. It wasn't a physical response, but just as Andres had caught the tremble in his voice, he saw this as well. Phillip seemed to falter a bit, to pull inside himself, then the moment passed, almost, it seemed, before it had happened.

He tilted his head toward the double doors behind them that led to the operating room. "How long have they been in there?"

Forever.

Andres glanced at his watch. "An hour and a half."

Bering spoke for the first time. He lived in his father's shadow, never quite measuring up, never quite making the grade. He compensated for this with a blustery attitude and a burning desire to replace his father in the practice. "An hour and a half? And no one's been out with an update?" He shook his head at Andres's obvious lack of status, then turned to Stephen. "Go find somebody who knows what's going on. Get a doctor out here."

Phillip nodded his approval and Stephen scurried off through the crowd. Wearing a self-satisfied expression, Bering said something about coffee and bustled over to a small kitchenette in one corner of the room, Richard going with him, offering help. Andres remained where he was, his black eyes meeting Phillip's blue ones with the coldest of gazes. Something passed between them. It definitely wasn't a truce—the war between them was too involved for that to ever happen—but the moment was understood by them both. This wasn't the time or place.

Jeff broke the tension by moving up to where Andres stood. He extended his hand, then his eyes widened as Andres lifted his own, now swathed in bandages. "You were hit?" Jeff asked in surprise. "Why didn't you tell us—"

"No, no. I wasn't shot." He dismissed the inquiry with a shake of his head. When Carmen had arrived at the hospital with fresh clothes for him, she'd taken one look at his hand and forced him to have someone take care of it. He'd bruised three knuckles so badly the doctor had insisted on wrapping them. "It's nothing."

Behind him, Bering and Richard returned, Carmen helping them distribute the coffee they'd brought. Earlier Andres had been annoyed by her presence. Now he was glad. She handed out packets of sugar, then she made conversation and kept things cordial. Andres was suddenly grateful; he wasn't sure he could have kept up the facade for much longer.

Stephen returned with the doctor a moment later. They stepped to one side, isolated by a bumper of space from the waiting officers. "They're still in surgery," the man said, holding up his hands as if to ward off their questions. He was young but looked exhausted, his jaw dark with stubble, his shoulders a weary slump beneath his pristine white coat. "I'm Dr. Maness, Dr. Edwardson's assistant. She's still operating. The bullet's currently lodged in the diaphragm behind the patient's lung on the left side. It nicked the lobe before it stopped."

His gaze went to Phillip, then on to the other men until it came to Andres. Despite Phillip's age and obvious status, the doctor seemed to sense Andres was the man he should be addressing. Andres hardly noticed this, though. All he felt was a rush of anxiety as their eyes met and locked.

"I'm sorry," the doctor continued. "You're just going to have to be patient. If you want something to do, then go downstairs." He let his gaze go over all of them this time. He wore thick glasses and his eyes were bleary and sad behind them. "There's a cafeteria...and a chapel."

ANDRES DIDN'T LOOK for either place. He certainly wasn't hungry and he'd given up searching for comfort from above a long time ago. Instead he went outside. He wanted isolation and some distance from the crowd upstairs, stopping first at the hospital gift shop to buy a pack of cigarettes. He hadn't smoked in as many years as he hadn't prayed, but the craving had hit him and there was nothing to do but satisfy it.

Cupping his bandaged hand around the flame of his match, he was lighting the first one when Carmen opened the door of the hospital's atrium. As she walked across the flagstones toward him, he jumped to his feet, his pulse suspended in midbeat. She shook her head as soon as she saw him and motioned for him to sit back down.

"There's no news," she said. "I just came outside for some air." She stared curiously at the cigarette between his thumb and forefinger. "What are you doing? You don't smoke."

He was angry at seeing Phillip McKinney, angry over Lena's injury and angry at himself. With a pointed disregard for Carmen's feelings, Andres unleashed the emotion and sent it flying toward her, his words scathing. "You don't know me that well, Carmen. Don't tell me what I do and what I don't do.''

She blinked at his tone, and he immediately felt like a bastard. Instead of apologizing, he turned his face away from her and took a deep drag on the cigarette. The acrid smoke seared his lungs with a sting so painful it brought a wave of dizziness with it as well.

Without saying a word, she sat down on the concrete bench beside him. They weren't the only ones in the small, walled garden. There were other smokers who'd been banished, and they all wore the same worried expressions. No one saw the carefully tended flowers or heard the bubbling fountain. Andres studied a young man on the other side of the patio, his hand on the head of a young girl who was dancing a doll along the edge of a low concrete wall.

The silence between he and Carmen built and hung, then finally she spoke softly, almost reluctantly, it sounded to Andres. "This woman who was shot. Lena McKinney...you know her, don't you? From before. You didn't just meet today.''

It took him a moment to decide how to answer, then he realized there was only one way. He had to tell her the truth; she deserved it.

"Yes, I know Lena." He looked at the cigarette between his fingers. "I know her very well.''

"Why didn't you tell me before?''

"I didn't think it was important.''

She shifted on the bench. He could feel her eyes on him. "You didn't think it was important?" She shook her head and smiled softly. "That usually means it's just the opposite."

"Carmen…"

She stopped him. "You don't owe me an explanation, Andres."

"No." He rose abruptly. "I do owe you that. At least." He took a final, death-defying drag on the cigarette, then crushed it under his shoe. He turned and looked at her. "Lena and I were engaged at one time. We were going to marry."

"To marry!" Her dark eyes widened in surprise. "You mean she was your fiancée?"

"That's right."

"Wh-what happened? Why didn't you get married?"

"It didn't work out." His tone defied her to ask for more information. "I went back to Miami."

"And?"

"And what? That was it."

"You never saw her again?"

"Not until this morning."

Carmen sat immobile on the bench, a pinprick of guilt stinging Andres as he looked at her. He should never have slept with her. She wasn't crying, but she looked as if she wanted to. Beneath her expression, there was a gentle dignity that made him feel even worse.

"Does she still love you?"

Back in the plane, Lena's gaze had held nothing but disgust when she'd looked at him, yet she'd protected him with her life and now she might have to pay up. Did that mean she loved him or had she just been doing her job? He didn't know…so he didn't answer.

"I guess that wasn't the right question, was it?" Carmen asked.

His hand suddenly ached, a striking, sharp pain that bypassed the painkiller the doctor had insisted he take. He cradled the injured fingers with his other palm. "What do you mean?"

"I should have asked, 'Do *you* still love her?'"

This time she waited even longer for his answer. When it was obvious he wasn't going to reply, she stared at him a minute more, then she stood and walked away. He watched her disappear through the hospital door, and after it closed behind her, he reopened the package of cigarettes and tapped out another one. When he lit the end, the match trembled in his hand.

TWENTY MINUTES LATER, the double glass doors opened once more. Dropping his cigarette, Andres jumped to his feet again, his heart pounding as Jeff McKinney crossed the small patio and came in his direction.

The nearby ashtray was overflowing with butts, and Andre's stomach felt sour and sick. With nothing else to do, he'd been on his cell phone ever since Carmen had left, making calls and getting as much information as he could about what had happened. It hadn't taken long and the news had started a train of thought Andres couldn't stop. But those thoughts fled now.

"The nurse just found us," Jeff announced as he reached Andres's side. "The doctor's finished the surgery and she's coming out to talk to everyone."

"Did she say anything else? How'd it go? Is Lena okay—"

Jeff held up his hand and stopped him. "I don't know any more than what I just told you. Let's go upstairs and see what the doctor says—"

Andres was heading for the door before the young attorney could even finish. Jeff caught up with him a second later, sending a quick glance at the phone in Andres's hand. "Did you find out any more details?"

Andres nodded grimly. Normally, he wouldn't tell a civilian anything, but Jeff was an attorney. He knew the system. "According to Lena's right-hand man—some guy named Bradley—the shooter never made it off the field."

"Who was he?"

"They don't know yet."

"And your associate?"

"Potter's dead."

They walked into the hospital lobby. "How'd

this guy get in the airport?'' Jeff asked. ''With Lena in charge, I can't imagine—''

''Bradley wasn't sure, but he thinks the perp picked one of the baggage handlers and started a friendship. The bad guy had on the handler's ID and uniform and when they started checking afterward, they found the handler's body back at his apartment. Bradley thinks the guy might have hidden his weapon the day before when he visited his pal.''

Jeff raised his eyebrows. ''That's an awful lot to know so soon.''

''I wouldn't expect any less from Lena's team.'' Andres spotted the elevators and headed toward them, still speaking. ''Her sniper took out the shooter with a cold shot.'' He pointed to the base of his neck.

''Lena won't like that. She hates it when the snipers have to fire.''

Andres met Jeff's eyes with a steady look. ''I think she'll understand this time.''

The elevator came and they both got in.

''Before you got here, Lena had said there might be trouble with some group named the Red Tide. Was he a member?''

''That's the assumption.'' Andres shook his head angrily and jabbed at the buttons as he spoke. ''These *pendejos*—these Red Tide people—they're idiots. That makes them even more dangerous. We can't predict what they're going to do. They haven't actually done anything violent like this since—''

When Andres didn't continue, Jeff looked at him then obviously thought better of whatever question he'd had in mind. The silent elevator rose slowly. "Why do they want you dead?" Jeff asked finally.

"Because I'm trying to stop them and have been for years. They're behind ninety per cent of the drug shipments coming through here. They finance their political activities—their little riots and rigged elections—with drug money. They tell the people they're fighting for freedom when what they're really doing is taking it instead.''

"Drugs? I thought Lena said they were revolutionaries.''

"That's what they want everyone to think. They're nothing but a bunch of thugs, though.'' Andres paused, the inevitable conclusion he'd come to while he'd been waiting forming itself into words. "They've gone too far this time.''

The elevator pinged softly, announcing its arrival on the surgical floor. When the doors slid open, Andres held them back, but instead of walking out, he turned and looked at Jeff. His voice was low and soft. No one overhearing them would have even bothered to listen.

"Shooting Lena was the biggest mistake they could ever make,'' he said quietly. "I'll lock up every one of the bastards...or I'll die trying. *Ya están muertos.*''

Jeff stared at him, then nodded his head with a slow thoughtful movement. The Spanish needed no translation.

THE SURGEON came out moments later. She was a handsome woman, in her fifties, with graying hair and dark blue eyes that looked both kind and exhausted. She wore a set of green scrubs with her name embroidered on the left side. Laura Edwardson, M.D. Obviously recognizing Phillip as he held out his hand, she greeted him then nodded toward the rest of the group.

Her eyes stopped on Andres when she saw his bandaged hand. "You were the one who was with her?"

"That's right."

"She kept asking about you. Fought the anesthetic so hard I didn't think we'd ever get her out." Before he could reply, she continued. "She's in stable condition right now. The bullet clipped the lower lobe of her lung. We sutured that as best we could and put in a chest tube, but we're going to have to watch that area very closely. Infection can be a big problem in the lungs. So can pneumonia."

"We need a specialist."

She glanced at Phillip as he spoke. "That's exactly what I recommend," she said calmly. "In fact, I've already called in our thoracic man and our pulmonary man as well. Dr. Weingarten, the thoracic surgeon, assisted me in the operation, and he'll be monitoring her closely.'' She stood wearily. ''She'll be out of the recovery unit in an hour. After that, she'll be in intensive care until we know we're clear on that lung. Once she's settled into ICU, one of you can see her then. *One* of you.'' She paused until all eyes were on her. ''It's none of my business, but since she asked for Mr. Casimiro, I suggest it be him.''

SHE WAS COLD, colder than she'd ever been in her entire life, and nothing but a jumble of sounds and impressions made their way through the bone-chilling numbness. Lena lay perfectly still and let the sounds wash over her. Eventually one stood out—a bubbling noise. She had no idea what it was or where it came from, but strangely enough she was breathing in rhythm with it. Other than that, she felt little. It was like being suspended in mid-air, as if nothing were touching her, nothing holding her down, nothing holding her up. She wanted to open her eyes but she couldn't. Her lids were too heavy and when she tried to speak, her tongue felt the same way. Someone had attached weights to it.

Out of the confusion another detail started to register. It was minor, but she concentrated on it and tried to magnify the feeling. After a moment, she put a name to it. Touch. Someone was touching her. It took another second to understand where the connection was being made and another second after that to name it. Her hand. Someone was touching her hand. She strained to respond, but her fingers wouldn't move, the command never making it out from her brain.

"Lena...*querida*... Can you hear me?"

The words were soft in her ear, soft and loving. They brushed her cheek with a feathery touch and a warmth she craved. For some unexplained reason, the Spanish made her feel good, too, made her feel as though whoever had spoken cared deeply, cared passionately. Who was talking to her like this? She could hear the emotion in his voice and the coldness faded, if only for a moment. When he spoke again, she fought the cloud of confusion that surrounded her, but it was too strong. It picked her up and carried her off.

The last word she heard was *querida*. The last thing she felt was a kiss.

CHAPTER FOUR

HER SKIN WAS the color of pearls, a luminescent ivory so pale and bloodless Andres felt as if he were looking through Lena instead of at her. Even her hair seemed to have lost its hue, the blond-streaked strands limp and dull on the pillow beneath her head. Only hours ago, he realized with a start, she'd stood before him on the plane, vital and beautiful. Now she appeared as if all the energy in her body had drained out, and with it, her life.

He knew this wasn't the case. The doctor had reassured him that Lena would be fine. Her wounds seemed grievous, but she'd recover; they weren't fatal. Andres couldn't help himself, though. Myriad tubes and lines snaked from her body to the control panel above her bed, and his eyes darted to the monitor situated there. Along with other functions he knew nothing about, the apparatus apparently tracked her heartbeat, a path of peaks and valleys being traced on the amber-colored screen. Each time the red line dipped, he held himself still until it jerked back up.

He'd thought she was awake at first, when he'd

spoken in her ear, but now he wasn't sure. She lay motionless under the cotton blanket. All he could do was stare helplessly at her and feel his rage growing. It should have been him lying there.

Without warning, he thought of the night before the wedding, the last time they'd been together while she'd still loved him. He could even remember what she'd worn that evening. A dark-blue dress, clingy, sexy, with tiny sparkles all over it. She'd had sandals that matched, two straps of navy leather and little else. The shoes and the short hem had shown off her tanned legs and the color had deepened the gray in her eyes. The outfit wasn't her usual style, but she'd told him she'd seen it in a shop window in Pensacola and it'd made her think of him and of the Caribbean. She'd been so excited about the honeymoon she'd talked about it more than the wedding.

Lena moaned softly, a painful sound that sliced right into his heart. Andres leaned over the bed, taking her hand in his. Her fingers felt like ice and he rubbed them gently to warm them, wishing he could do more, but knowing he couldn't.

"I'm here, *querida*... I'm here."

FROM THE HALLWAY, there were windows into the patients' rooms and during visiting hours, the blinds were pulled back. Anyone passing by could see inside. Carmen watched carefully as Andres took Lena's hand. His movement was filled with emotion, his entire body straining with the effort of caring for her, listening to her…loving her.

It couldn't have been more obvious had he stood up and shouted it to the world, she thought. He still loved Lena McKinney. The part he held back from everyone else, including her, he gave to Lena and probably always had. Carmen felt a wave of anger and resentment wash over her. He'd taken advantage of her and she'd let him.

She stared, her bitterness etching its way deeper inside her psyche, then she turned away from the glass and walked down the hall.

TUESDAY MORNING, Lena woke up slowly. Her mouth was dry, her throat parched, but for the first time, her mind felt clear. Even though the nurses had already gotten her up and forced her to walk, for some reason, she was more aware of her surroundings than she had been previously. They'd pulled the chest tube, too, an unpleasant experience to say the least. She'd drifted through most of that, wishing she were somewhere else.

Her eyes followed the lines of the room until they came to the chair in the corner. She wasn't sure why, but she'd expected to see Andres. Instead, her father was dozing in the wingback, his head tilted against the padded side.

She studied him for a moment. She'd never noticed that his hair was so thin or his wrists so bony and white. Had her accident affected him that much or had she simply never taken the time to truly look? Shaken, she started to sit up, then gasped as a lightning strike of pain hit her lower chest.

The sound woke him, and Phillip rose immediately, his eyes widening as he saw her pain-etched face. He was at her bedside in a heartbeat. "Lena? Baby? What's wrong? Do you need the doctor?"

He hadn't used that term of endearment in years, and the sound of it now made her grin weakly. "Hey, Daddy..." she croaked. Each word was painful, each breath torture...but not as much as it had been. "Could I just have some water?"

He reached for a nearby pitcher and poured her a glass, then helped her drink through the straw. "You look better," he said, staring down at her with a critical eye. "Are you sore? How's the incision?" The questions came as rapidly as a cross-examination. "Can you breathe all right?"

"Don't you have something better to do than sit here and bother me?" she asked hoarsely.

"Not at the moment, no."

After the death of Dorothea McKinney, Lena's mother, Lena and her father had become very close, each depending on the other for love and support. They'd grown apart through the years as Phillip had become too controlling, and the relationship had changed into a seesaw of love and manipulation. His violent opposition to Andres had pushed Lena away even more. But seeing him here now, sitting in her hospital room when she knew he had work to do made Lena feel like a little girl again, loved and protected.

The emotion lasted only a second. Sensing her regained strength, he spoiled the moment with his very next words.

"What in the *hell* did you think you were doing, Lena?" He knit his eyebrows together in one angry line as he set her cup back down. "You could have gotten yourself killed out there! And for what? I can't believe you let yourself do this—"

Lena tuned the words out, just as she did each time her father acted this way. He was the only person on the planet she let talk to her so disrespectfully. She would have crucified any of her team if they'd dared do the same.

After he ran out of steam, Lena defended herself. "I was doing the job I'm paid to do," she answered. "I'm a cop, Daddy. And I'll always be a cop."

His lips were a firm line, and she knew what part of the argument was coming next. He had begged her to go to law school, to join her brothers at the firm, but she'd wanted to be a policewoman. "Nonsense! There's plenty of time for you to go back to school. You could walk into the firm and be a partner in no time."

"Daddy…"

He ignored her warning tones. "You're too damned bright to waste your talents on that rinky-dink police force. You could do so much better. If I've told you once—"

"You've told me a thousand times," she interrupted, "and you *don't* need to tell me again. I know how you feel about it."

Her impudence brought out his old trump card. "Your mother would not have liked this."

The words usually wearied Lena, but somehow this time they did just the opposite. She pursed her mouth tightly, her lips the only part of her body she could move without causing pain.

"Then consider that *your* fault," she answered sharply. "You taught me there were things worth fighting for. *You* taught me the difference between right and wrong."

"The difference between right and wrong..." His stare was blue and piercing—Dorothea had been the one to give Lena the granite-gray eyes— and suddenly Lena understood they'd come to the heart of the argument. "Is that what you think you were doing when you saved Casimiro's life?"

He said the Spanish surname incorrectly. Time and time again, she'd told Phillip how to say Andres's last name, but he insisted on his way. Finally she'd realized he was deliberately trying to denigrate Andres by mispronouncing his name, and she'd given up trying to rectify the mistake.

He spoke in a biting voice. "If that's what you think you were doing—"

"I was doing my job," she reiterated.

Not that she'd done it very well, she thought to herself. Each time she'd woken, that had been her only coherent thought. *She'd screwed up. Big time.* No unauthorized person should have been anywhere near that airport, and if she had been paying attention to her work instead of Andres, she wouldn't be in a hospital bed now.

"Well, I can't believe you almost got yourself killed for the likes of him. He isn't worth the time of day, much less your life. I don't want you having anything to do with him, Lena." His voice rose stridently, as if he were winding up a case. "You can't trust him and he'll hurt you again. Do you hear me?"

"Everyone can hear you. But it doesn't matter one way or the other. I have no intentions in that direction, I can assure you."

"I'm glad to see you've finally gotten some sense about the son of a bitch because I don't care how important he is, the man's still a worthless bastard."

With the last word ringing in the air, the door of Lena's room suddenly swung open…and Andres stood on the other side.

Lena's eyes swept over the man in the doorway. Dressed in a navy suit, his chiseled shoulders filling the opening, Andres held a crystal vase of Brazilian orchids, their petals snowy white and curved against the somber color of his jacket.

"Am I interrupting?"

His voice was reserved, polite even, but he'd heard what Phillip had said. Something in the set of his expression told her this and she was assaulted instantly by a complicated storm of emotions. She spoke quickly before her father could reply. "P-please come in, Andres. You're not interrupting a thing."

He walked inside and set the vase down on the table beside her. The faint, sweet smell of the flowers drifted over Lena's bed. When they'd been together, he'd always brought her orchids.

"They're beautiful," she said despite herself. "Thank you."

When he didn't reply, she looked up. Andres and her father were locked in a staring battle, the tension so fierce between the two of them Lena could almost see the cloud of pressure taking shape over her bed. She wasn't surprised since they'd always disliked each other, but there was something different in the air this time. Something thicker, denser.

Surprisingly, her father looked away first. He reached for the briefcase he'd left beside his chair, and spoke—to Lena only. "I have to get back to the office. If you need anything, you call me, baby."

She accepted his kiss on her forehead then watched him go out the door. He said nothing to Andres. Didn't even acknowledge his presence.

Her gaze went back to the man she'd almost

married. He stared at the closing door with a brow-marring frown that cleared only after he realized she was looking at him.

"What is it with you two?" she asked in exasperation.

"You don't really want to know."

"I wouldn't have asked if I didn't."

"Your father loves you," he said after a second. "Let's just leave it at that." He moved toward the window and looked outside before turning to speak again. "Tell me how you feel today."

"Better," she said automatically. His answer hadn't satisfied her. For a moment, she considered pursuing the topic, even though she knew Andres would say no more. Why on earth would there be even more animosity between the two men now? When Andres had left her at the altar, Phillip had gotten what he wanted.

"Better?" He raised one eyebrow. "*¿Verdad?*"

"Yes. I feel more clear, if that makes sense. Still sore, but more with it." She reached again for her water, but he did as well. Holding the plastic cup closer, his fingers over hers, he bent the straw toward her mouth. His touch was warm, his whole hand covering hers.

"I can do it myself," she said.

"I know that."

They stared at each other for a second, the same old sparks flying between them, heating her up. Lena took a deep breath and pulled the cup away.

He acted as if it didn't matter one way or the other, stepping back from the bed with a neutral expression.

Lena spoke quickly in an effort to cover up her reaction to his touch. "Has the P.D. found out anything about the shooter?"

"They know for sure the guy wasn't local. All his identification papers—driver's license, ATM card, whatever—were fake and his prints aren't coming up at all. They're examining the recent flights from the islands. Washington thinks he was probably brought in for the job."

"Washington?" Lena didn't bother to hide the surprise in her voice.

"The FBI."

"But the local guys can handle this—"

"And they are. They sent the prints to the feds as a precaution, just to widen their investigation. The FBI has a better database."

"What about the weapon? Where'd it come from?"

"They don't know yet. The serial number didn't come up stolen."

She inched upward in the bed, holding back a groan as a dull ache began to throb along her incision. "Tell Bradley I want to see him. I need to know what the department's doing about all this and then I want—"

Andres leaned down as she spoke and put his hands on the mattress, stilling her movement.

"You don't need to know anything, Lena. All you need to do is lie there and recover. Let the police department handle this. They're perfectly capable of being in charge—"

"But *I'm* in charge of the Emerald Coast SWAT team," she answered, bristling at his tone. "I may be temporarily out of action but I'm still the commander. I want to know what's going on."

"What's going on is that you're going to recuperate, and the P.D.'s going to investigate. That's all."

The response was typical Andres—Latin and arrogant. "In case you haven't noticed," she said slowly, "you have no authority here. I am responsible for this situation."

"I'm well aware of that fact," he said, surprising her. "But I understand something that apparently you do not."

"And that is?"

"You won't get well if you don't rest."

"That's my concern."

His voice was liquid and low. It rippled over her bed and made her pull up the blanket without thinking. "I care what happens to you."

"You don't have the right to care anymore," she said bluntly. "That time has passed."

"Maybe. Maybe not."

"No." She shook her head, his unexpected answer triggering something inside her. "There's no maybe to it, Andres," she answered. "Not anymore. When you left me two years ago, you left me. It's over and done with, and if you're thinking differently, then you're making a terrible mistake.''

ANDRES DEPARTED a few minutes later, and the last of Lena's energy evaporated in the aftermath of their exchange. What was he doing? What was he thinking? If he was considering a reconciliation, he was nuts. The world would have to come to an end before she'd ever get back together with Andres. Ever. To make matters worse, her father would be so opposed he'd make life hell for her. He hated Andres still, maybe even more than ever. She didn't understand why, but that much was very clear.

She shook her head, her hair whispering against her pillow. No...Lena had given Andres her heart and he'd walked away. He'd never get another chance to do that.

LENA DOZED then fell completely under, sleeping so deeply that neither sound nor light could penetrate the almost coma-like rest. When something finally broke through and woke her up late that afternoon, she opened her eyes and was momentarily shocked. Her bed was surrounded by men in black. Automatically she did a head count. Every one of her fifteen officers was standing over her and grinning. She remembered a couple of them visiting when she was still groggy, but seeing them all together was truly surprising.

"Who's minding the store?" she asked, without thinking.

They laughed at her characteristic remark. Bradley, the designated commander since the shooting, stepped forward to answer. "We told dispatch to hold it down," he said, his voice a low-pitched rumble in the confines of the crowded room. He was a gentle giant—a huge black officer with gray frosting his close-cut hair. "Told 'em they couldn't be havin' any emergencies for at least twenty minutes...."

She eased up in the bed and winced. "And you think the bad guys are going to listen?"

"They'd better." From the back of the room, Peter Douglas, one of the rear entry men spoke up. "If they know what's good for them!"

Beck Winters stepped through the crowd to stand beside Lena's bed. He was one of the men she recalled visiting her, his very pregnant wife, Jennifer, in tow. He looked down at Lena now. "We really want you to hurry up and get back to work. Bradley's way too easygoing and we're afraid we might lose our edge without you around. Our workouts are going downhill and training...forget about it!"

"I *could* direct you guys from here. I don't want you getting fat and happy without me around...."

The men chuckled and looked embarrassed, but

underneath their studied reactions, their relief at Lena's recovery was palpable. They respected her and even though she was harsh at times, they were proud of their unit. It went unsaid that no one wanted to lose a member, especially a leader. They were a family as much as a team.

"Since you're all here, I just want to let you know that I think you did a great job the other day," Lena said when the laughter died. "Things didn't go exactly as we planned, but once it went down, the whole team reacted perfectly. I'm proud of every one of you."

They murmured protests at her praise, but she waved their words aside. "I'm telling you the truth," she said. "Everyone did what was supposed to be done, and we accomplished our main goal. I think you should all be happy with your work."

They visited a little bit longer, then one by one the officers said their goodbyes and left. On duty twenty-four hours a day, the team trained and took classes when they weren't responding to calls. It was a difficult life, and hard as hell on their families. Sarah had to have performed a miracle for all of them to come in and see Lena at once. She watched them leave and thought about how lucky she was to have such a good group of people around her.

Beck and Bradley remained behind. She questioned Bradley closely about the situation. The team never investigated the call-outs that sent them running, but they always stayed on top of the cases. It gave closure to their actions and fostered a sense of accomplishment when the issues were resolved. Bradley gave her the same answers Andres had. Except for one important detail. Bradley was sure the shooter had been a member of the Red Tide organization. The weapon, his nationality, even his method—they all pointed to the group who wanted Andres dead.

Bradley left a few minutes after that, promising to keep her informed. As the door closed behind the huge officer, Beck turned back to her.

"You're looking pretty good." Towering over her bed, he was tall as a Norse god and just as imposing. His blond hair was cropped short, his muscles long and lean. They'd been co-workers for a long time, friends even longer. Lena would be the godmother to his baby when it arrived.

"I'm feeling much better," she said.

"When will you get back to work?"

She grimaced. "I'm not sure. They'll probably let me out in a few days, then the docs say I'll have a couple more weeks taking it easy before I can return. When I finally do get there, I may not be able to go out right off."

"You'll need to take care of yourself."

She rolled her eyes. "Please, I don't need anyone else giving me advice like that today. I've had more than enough."

He grinned, but his gaze held sympathy. "Your father?"

"No..." She cursed herself for saying anything, but it was too late to stop now. She had to explain. "Andres."

Beck's expression shifted. He'd liked Andres a lot, but he'd also been a witness to Lena's pain after the relationship was over. She knew his reaction to the news would be a mixed one.

"He's giving you advice?" was all Beck said.

"He gives advice to everyone."

"But are you taking it?"

She lifted her gaze to Beck's. His eyes were chips of blue ice, the total opposite to Andres's simmering black ones. "He told me I needed to rest," she said. "That I should let Bradley run the show and just worry about getting well."

"He's right."

"He also said he's concerned about me."

"Concerned, eh?" The blue gaze deepened. "And how do you feel about him? That bullet did have his name on it, you know. Does that bother you?"

"I have no feelings for Andres whatsoever. He no longer matters to me. I truly don't care."

Beck looked at her steadily as her last words died. "A simple no would have worked," he finally said.

She started to shoot back an answer, but nothing came. Beck was right, as usual. She should have just said no and left it at that. But when Andres was involved, she went over the top, one way or the other.

Beck left a little later and she eased over in the bed to stare out the window. She told herself her reaction meant nothing, but the words rang hollowly...even in her mind.

CHAPTER FIVE

AT THE END OF THE WEEK, Lena sat on the edge of her hospital bed and fidgeted as the doctor listened to her chest and tapped her on the back. "Another breath, please."

She drew in as deeply as she could, then let the air out slowly. She remained sore and uncomfortable but the piercing pain of the first few days had finally disappeared. She was ready to leave and had told the doctor so more than once.

After a moment of listening, the physician stepped away from the bed, her stethoscope in her hands. "I'm going to have Dr. Weingarten look at you this afternoon and if he agrees, then we'll discharge you." Dr. Edwardson's voice was full of warning. "But you may not go back to work for at least two full weeks, and I'd prefer that you waited longer than that. You need to give yourself plenty of time. Nothing strenuous for at least a month and a half."

Lena nodded, visions of her own bed, her own bath, her own set of sheets dancing in her head. She couldn't wait to get back to the rickety old house. A lot of confusing thoughts were parading through her brain, and she needed the solace of her beachfront home. She did her best thinking on the deck looking out over the water. And God knew she needed to do some thinking.

Andres was *still* in town and showed no signs of leaving. She'd asked him why he hadn't returned to Miami, but he'd simply given her his standard Latin answer, a shrug of his broad shoulders, and changed the subject. She couldn't figure out what he was doing and it was driving her crazy.

She pulled her hospital gown back up over her shoulders and focused on the woman beside the bed. "Thanks for everything," she said.

"You're very welcome." The physician slipped her stethoscope back into her pocket and smiled. "But try not to come back. We don't like repeat customers."

The gray-haired woman left a moment later, and Lena walked slowly to the door to follow her out. Her side was stiff and sore, but the more she moved, the better it felt. The physical therapist had shown her how to stretch and work her injured muscles, and twice a day she shuffled to the other end of the hospital wing for extra exercise. She began the long walk now, each step bringing her a little more flexibility.

Ten minutes later she was standing by the window of the ward housing the newborns. Somehow she always ended up here. Leaning her hands against the window, Lena looked at the babies.

There were only two today, one wrapped in a blue blanket, the other in pink. The day before there had been twins in another set of the beds, each bundled up in blue covers, their tiny heads fuzzed with black down, their legs and arms kicking in protest as the nurses tended to them. Lena had felt the old familiar longing deep inside her.

She wore a gun to work, but that didn't make her different from other women; she still wanted children, a husband, a home. She'd never told anyone how much she wanted children—in a SWAT team environment that subject didn't come up much—but she had confided in Andres. He'd assured her he wanted a large family, too, and she'd been thrilled. Imagining what their children would look like, she'd come up with perfect images each time. A little blond girl who looked just like her and a boy, all boy, of course, who was a miniature Andres.

After she and Andres had parted, Lena had set aside those dreams and had even refused to date for a long time. But Beck had started on her, and tired of his ragging, she'd given in and begun to go out again. There was no shortage of men when you worked with cops but none of them had provided more than passing entertainment. She'd dated Nate Allen, the police chief of Pensacola for quite some time, but she'd finally had to tell him it might be best for them both to call it off. He'd been terribly hurt, and she'd felt like a four-letter word, but what else could she do? The relationship had been doomed from the very start and she'd known it all along.

One of the babies started to cry. Lena couldn't hear the child through the thick glass, but she could see his open mouth as his face turned red and his tiny body began to shake in his bassinet. A nurse quickly appeared to soothe him, picking him up and patting his tiny shoulders. Lena watched for as long as she could stand it, then she headed back to her room.

LEANING AGAINST the doorway of the hospital room, Andres watched Lena walk down the hall. She didn't know he was observing her because she was completely focused on her progress. It was steady, but clearly painful as she took step after careful step on the spotless linoleum.

She'd lost at least ten pounds, ten pounds she couldn't afford to lose, and beneath her light-blue robe, her finely toned body looked thin and fragile. Even her face looked slimmer, her cheekbones more pronounced, her jawline finer. He continued to examine her until she finally felt his gaze and looked up. Her expression, a study in concentration, changed immediately to one of guarded wariness.

Andres started down the corridor, stopping only

when he reached her side. He couldn't help himself; he took her elbow, his fingers wrapping around her arm. "Let me help you."

"Thank you," she said firmly. "But it's better if I make it on my own. I need to do it myself." She pulled her arm away from his touch just as she had the day he'd tried to help her with her water.

Her reaction stung even though it wasn't unexpected. Lena was the most independent woman he knew. "I guess it's true what they say...some things never change, no?"

Her eyes narrowed. "What's that supposed to mean?"

"You know exactly what it means." He spoke calmly, rationally even, but inside he was a wreck. "You never need anyone."

She gathered the collar of her robe and pulled it closer. "There's nothing wrong with being self-reliant."

"No, there isn't. But there's nothing wrong with accepting help, either. You might give it a try sometime, Lena."

Without answering him, she resumed her walking, her gait more stiff than it had been a moment before, a result of their conversation more than her injury. A brittle silence filled the space between them.

"I just talked with Dr. Edwardson." Digging up his patience, Andres tried to break the tension once more. "She told me she's probably going to release you this afternoon. I'll come back at five to pick you up.''

Lena stopped again, so abruptly this time, he thought something was really wrong. There was, he realized a moment later, but not with her body.

"That won't be necessary. I can—"

"Don't be ridiculous, Lena. Let me take you home."

"You don't need to do that." She spoke through gritted teeth. "My father can drive me if I don't want to call a taxi."

They were standing outside her room, near the nurses' station. Andres could feel their curious looks on his back. He lowered his voice and spoke again, before Lena could protest further as he knew she was about to do. "Let's go inside, shall we?"

She glanced over his shoulder, then nodded, walking inside ahead of him. He caught just a whiff of almonds as she passed. She still used the same shampoo. The realization distracted him and that, in turn, made him remember the conversation he'd had a few hours before with his boss.

"Are you sure this is a good decision, Casimiro? Have you thought it through?" The director had sounded worried.

"It's the only choice I have. I'm not leaving here until I've stopped these Red Tide *bastardos*. They may try again. Why should I endanger anyone else?"

"You could go back to the office in Miami. I

could give you twenty-four hour security with our guys. If we can get them up here, we can nail them.''

"I have a better chance of baiting them from Destin, of luring them in. There are good people running things down here and they can help me,'' Andres argued. "And as long as I'm here, I can take care of the operations that Potter was supposed to handle.''

The director had dropped his voice. "Andres, you can stay there and do that—hell, you can do anything you want to—but do you understand the consequences?''

"I understand. I still need to stay, though—''

As if Andres hadn't spoken, his boss continued. "You're on the fast track. There are people in Washington keeping their eyes on you, but if you disappear in some backward Florida town just to run an ops shop, your name is not going to be one that gets brought up in meetings. As much as I'd like to see you get these assholes, I don't want you to sacrifice your career for it. Do you understand what I'm saying?''

Andres had let the silence build, then he'd spoken. "This is something I have to do.''

The director sighed, a weary sound that told Andres exactly what kind of fool he thought he was. "All right then. You do what you have to do.''

The words reverberating in his mind, Andres looked across the room to Lena. She stood beside the foot of her bed. In spite of her obvious loathing of him, he'd couldn't leave Destin. Not now.

He owed it to Mateo to deal with these idiots.

He owed it to Lena, even though she didn't know it.

He owed it to himself.

Holding on to the metal railing with one hand, Lena spoke with vehemence. "I'm not sure I understand what's going on." Her knuckles were white where they gripped the runner. "I want an explanation, Andres."

He stared at her and remained silent.

"Why are you still here?" Her voice rose slightly when he didn't answer. It held a tremble as well. "What about your job? Why haven't you gone back to Miami? And give me a real answer, this time, not some shrug."

He took a deep breath and prepared himself for her reaction. She wasn't going to be happy with his news. "I didn't know what was going to happen and that's why I haven't said anything. But I talked to my director today, and there's been a change of plans."

She didn't move, didn't even blink.

"I'm not going back to Miami, Lena. I'm staying here. Here in Destin."

Her mouth fell open then she snapped it shut. "You can't do that."

"Potter's gone and there's no one else available to open the office."

"There's got to be someone else. You're not the only hotshot in the Justice Department."

"Hotshot, eh? Is that what you think I am?"

"That's the rumor."

"But not the truth?"

"I don't know, but I don't care, either." She moved closer to him, as if her proximity would make her point stronger. "I do know one thing, though. There are other men who could run this shop. If you're staying here, you have a reason. A real reason. I want to know what it is."

"This feels like an interrogation."

"Call it whatever you like. Just give me an answer."

He stepped away from her then, putting some distance between them by crossing the room to stand beside the window. The afternoon sun had disappeared behind a bank of stormy fall clouds. They were rolling in from the east. He watched them for a few moments, gathering his thoughts. He should have known better than to try to protect her. She didn't need him and she definitely didn't need that.

"I want to catch these bastards, Lena," he said. Turning around once more, he faced her. It was the truth, after all. Part of it, anyway.

"We've never known where the main cell was. Because of the amount of drugs we're seeing locally and their attempt at the airport, it could very well be here in Destin. If I stay, I might force their hand."

"Force their hand?" Her voice was incredulous. "Don't you think they're aggressive enough as it is?"

"They've got to be stopped."

"And they will be. The Destin P.D. can do it."

"I'm not saying they can't. But if I stay here—"

"If you stay here, you'll just make things more difficult." Her jaw twitched angrily. "You know this isn't the way to get this done so why are you making it harder for us?"

"I'm not trying to do that," he said. "But I can't just walk away. Not now."

She stared at him. Her eyes matched the clouds outside, but as he watched, the dark gray grew even more wintry. "What happened to me is my concern. Not yours. It's part of the job and you know that as well as I do. I'll handle it on my own." Her mouth turned down, into a bitter line. "It's something I've grown accustomed to doing in the past two years."

As always, she managed, with one swift jab, to cut straight to the chase.

His abandonment had inflicted a wound on her that everyone saw, that everyone could comprehend. Until he could tell her the whole truth—and he didn't see that ever happening—the injury would never heal.

"We should sit down and talk." He would think

of something to tell her. "There are things that need to be explained...."

She interrupted him. "All I want is to be left alone. If you're staying here out of some kind of misguided guilt, you're making a big mistake. You don't owe me anything, and I don't want you here."

He looked into her eyes and his chest tightened. He didn't have a choice. There was only one way he could answer her and only one thing he could do.

"I'm sorry, but you're not going to get what you want, Lena. I'm staying here. And you have nothing to say about it."

RIGHT AFTER LUNCH, Dr. Weingarten, the thoracic surgeon, came in and after looking Lena over again, released her with warnings about doing too much. She barely heard the doctor. All she could think of was Andres's news.

He was staying in Destin.

Why? Why now? Why did he have to come back after all this time?

Angrily grabbing the phone beside the bed, she dialed her father's office and asked for Jeff.

Her thoughts were still in a turmoil when her younger brother walked into her hospital room a half hour later to take her home.

They were halfway to her house, the windows of the Toyota down, the cold sea air washing in as they puttered down Highway 98, before Jeff took a chance and spoke. When they'd been kids, her temper had been legendary. She might have been the girl, but all her brothers had been scared of her.

He looked at her from across the seat. "What's going on? I thought Andres was taking you home. He told me last night he wanted to see if—"

"Andres Casimiro doesn't always get what he wants." Turning in the seat with a slight grimace, Lena interrupted her little brother, belatedly realizing she'd used the same phrase Andres had spoken to her a few hours before. "Did you know he's staying here?" she demanded. "To run the ops shop?"

Jeff's surprised expression revealed his answer before he even spoke. "I didn't know that," he replied after a moment. "But I guess it makes sense now that I think about it...."

"No, it doesn't," she insisted. "He has no business here. He said he wants to draw out the Red Tide, but that's ridiculous. We can catch those guys without him here."

Jeff steered the car around a slow-moving construction truck. "Of course, you can," he said. "But that's not really why he's staying and you know it."

A ray of sunshine had broken through the clouds and hit the water to their right. Lena had been watching the waves, but when Jeff spoke, she quickly swung her gaze back to him.

"Andres and I talked while you were in surgery. He said the men who shot you were *ya están muertos*. Does that give you a hint?"

Lena felt a sudden chill that had nothing to do with the open window beside her. "*Ya están muertos?* Are you sure?"

"'Already dead.'" Jeff nodded. "That's what it means, right?"

She didn't answer because she didn't know what to say. Those were strong words. What had fueled them?

She thought about it until they pulled into her driveway, Jeff carefully maneuvering around the ruts in the shell road to bring them right in front of the door. He killed the engine and looked at her. Faintly, Lena heard the waves hitting the beach. Other than that, there was total silence.

Her brother spoke. "He was really shaken up, Lena. I don't know if you know it or not, but he put his fist through the wall at the hospital. He almost broke three fingers. He was madder than hell and he still is. He wants to get these guys."

Her chest went tight. "'Getting these guys' is not his job."

"Well, he thinks it is."

She shook her head. "He's forgetting who he works for. The Justice Department doesn't investigate local homicide attempts."

"This doesn't have anything to do with who he works for."

She stared at Jeff. "What are you saying?"

"They shot you, Lena. Don't you realize what that means?"

She put her hand on the bandage beneath her blouse. "I think I've got a pretty good idea—"

"No. No, you don't. This is personal. It's got nothing to do with work. Andres still cares about you."

Jeff was so naive she wondered sometimes how he could actually practice law. He lived in a parallel universe, she thought. A perfect one where everyone lived happily ever after. "You're nuts."

"Am I? There are a thousand guys in Washington who could handle this office. Why him?"

As her brother repeated the very same words she'd said to Andres, Lena bit her bottom lip and remembered his answer. *I can't just walk away. Not after what happened to you.*

When she didn't answer, Jeff spoke again. "Lena, he still cares about you."

"No, he doesn't. He can't."

"If you'd seen him waiting while they were operating on you... He was a wreck."

"That doesn't mean anything."

Her brother waited a few seconds then he spoke again, almost with distraction. "Look, I know you two had a rocky time before, but Andres is not leaving until he finds the men responsible for your shooting." He gripped the steering wheel. "He won't go back to Miami until the job is done or someone stops him.''

All she could do was shake her head. An hour later, Jeff left. She watched him drive away, his words in her mind. Deep, deep down, where she didn't go too often, she wondered if Jeff could be right, but as soon as she formed the question, she put it away.

Andres didn't still love her.

He couldn't.

CHAPTER SIX

CARMEN HAD ARRANGED the Monday luncheon, and the minute Andres walked into the restaurant, he wished he'd told her to have sandwiches delivered instead. He'd wanted to meet the office staff Zack Potter had assembled and give them the news that he'd be taking over, but he wanted to do it in a way that didn't upset anyone any more than they already were. The restaurant was packed. How was he going to talk to everyone in this setting?

Carmen read his mind as she saw him come through the door and into the noisy waiting room. Gently pushing through the crowd, she took his arm and pulled him to one side. "There's a private room in the back," she said. "It's quiet, and no one will bother us. In fact, just about everyone is there already."

He nodded and began to trail her through the restaurant, then he stopped abruptly. Carmen stopped as well, looking at him with a puzzled expression.

"Andres?"

Her voice died out as she followed his gaze.

From across the busy dining room, Phillip McKinney had obviously witnessed their arrival and was making his way to where they waited. Each step was purposeful, and his stare never wavered from Andres's face.

When Andres had shown up at the hospital Friday evening to take Lena home, she'd already left. He hadn't spoken to her since but he had no doubt Phillip had whisked her away before Andres could get there. Her father probably wanted to gloat.

Andres watched the silver-haired man stride toward him. *Had* he arranged Mateo's death? *Was* he involved with the Red Tide? The hatred Andres had always felt for Phillip was as much a part of his life as breathing; giving up the investigation to prove Phillip's guilt had been one of the hardest decisions Andres had ever made.

Now, once again he found himself second-guessing that choice. Phillip might be older but he was no less the man he had been. If he wanted Andres dead nothing would be able to stop him. On the other hand, would he put his own daughter in danger to accomplish his goal?

It was all so twisted, Andres thought, so tangled up. Lena, her father...the past. From the minute Andres had seen her in the airplane, he'd felt himself drawn to her again. The emotional upheaval of her shooting had overshadowed his true feelings, but they couldn't be contained any longer. The decision to stay here had as much to do with her as it did anything. Andres wasn't the kind of man who'd try to fool himself into thinking otherwise. He still had to sort through everything and decide what it all meant, but Phillip was a complication he could have done without.

The attorney halted his progress directly in front of Andres, his expression bordering on the belligerent, his stance almost aggressive.

Andres turned to Carmen before Lena's father could say anything. "Tell the group to go ahead and order their lunch. I'll be right there."

She looked uncertain, but he nodded toward the dining room. "I'll only be a minute."

She shot Phillip an unreadable look, then started toward the back of the dining room, her high heels clicking on the shining terrazzo floor. Andres faced Phillip. "What can I do for you to—"

"Is it true?" he interrupted rudely. "Are you taking Potter's place?"

Andres lifted one eyebrow. "You're either well connected or you've talked to Lena. Which one is it?"

Phillip answered the question by asking one of his own. "She knows?"

"I told her on Friday," Andres answered. "And yes, I am taking Potter's place. I'll be running the operations here, at least for a while."

Phillip wasted no time. "You stay away from my daughter. I don't want you around her. At all."

"I think that's a decision for Lena and me to make."

"You broke her heart once already. I won't have you hurting her again."

"She's a grown woman."

"Who's vulnerable and wounded. It was bad enough for you to show up in Destin, but to ask her to protect your sorry life—"

"Just a minute, *viejo*." Andres's voice went soft as he looked at Phillip with a cold expression. "You'd better watch what you're saying."

Phillip McKinney's blue eyes didn't waver in the sunlight pouring through a nearby window. "I love my daughter. I want you to stay away from her."

"Or what?" Andres asked, suddenly taking a chance. "You'll 'take care' of things like you tried to before? It didn't work then, Phillip, and it won't work now. Save your breath if that's what you're doing."

"I was protecting her."

All at once, Andres realized they were talking about two different things. He'd been thinking of Mateo and the old man had been remembering the money. Andres had almost forgotten that issue— it'd been so insignificant to him.

He laughed. "You were protecting her. Of course. That's why you told Lena what you did." He smoothed a hand down his tie, then looked up, straight into Phillip's eyes. "You *have* told her, haven't you? That you offered me a half a million to leave her alone?'' *And when that didn't work, you tried to kill me.*

Phillip flinched, his face taking on an uncharacteristic slackness. "She didn't need to know about that. And it...it's in the past now."

"And you want it to stay that way, don't you?"

"Y-yes. I do." He started to bluster. "There's no reason to tell Lena, and even if I did, it wouldn't matter. She'd understand."

"She'd understand...." Andres shook his head. "She may be your flesh and blood, Phillip, but you don't know the first thing about your daughter if you believe she'd understand that."

He reached out and put his hand on the older man's shoulder. Anyone watching them would think they were having a pleasant conversation, two old friends, maybe discussing an upcoming fishing trip. If they looked close, though, they'd see the hard glint in Andres's eyes. It was anything but friendly.

"Your daughter is a grown woman, Señor McKinney. She's old enough, and smart enough, to make any decision on her own. Respect that for once and let her live her own life." He paused and let his words sink in. "If I were you, I'd worry about something more important than who my daughter was dating."

Phillip blinked and something undecipherable flashed across his face before he could hide it. Suddenly the whole conversation took on more meaning than it had before. Andres's gut rolled over once, then again.

"Nothing's more important than Lena," Phillip said.

"I hope you're telling the truth." Andres waited a second but Phillip stayed silent. "If you aren't, you'll regret it."

Phillip hesitated, then he turned on his heel and marched across the dining room. Andres watched him leave. Phillip was older, yes, and slower, maybe, but he still had a fire within him. He could prove dangerous yet.

Andres would have to watch his back.

LENA SPENT the first week out of the hospital regaining her strength.

She spent the second week going nuts.

Unable to drive, she'd been stuck at the house the whole time, nothing to occupy her but the television and family visits, most of which she could have done without. Her brothers and their wives had been sympathetic, but they lived such different lives from Lena it was hard to connect, especially with Bering. He was so far removed from who they'd been as children he was almost a stranger to her. He'd called once, alleging to check on her, but she'd suspected he had another reason, one she knew nothing about. He truly cared for no one; only money meant anything to him.

Lena finally turned to what she usually did for distraction; she went back to work, but only by phone. She had called Sarah so many times the information officer was having to think up things to talk to her about. Thank God Bradley did a little better. He took her twice-daily intrusions in stride and patiently updated her on everything the team was doing. The reports didn't really help Lena—all they did was make her more anxious to get back to work—but at least the conversations ate up a bit of the lonely time.

Saturday afternoon, puttering around on the deck, she suddenly stopped and stared out at the ocean. Was this what the rest of her life was going to be like? If she didn't marry and didn't have children, would she be living here and doing these same things in twenty years? Watering plants? Sweeping the floor? Counting the hours until she could go back to the station?

The thought depressed her, so she put it away and headed down the wooden planks to the beach as the afternoon drew to a close. She'd walked the stretch that morning already, but another mile wouldn't hurt.

She was halfway down the beach when she saw the blur of a large SUV speed by on the blacktop road that bordered the sand. She stood up straighter and shaded her eyes with one hand. Catching a quick glimpse of a tanned face and dark sunglasses, she instantly recognized the driver and the vehicle, and she knew the destination. Andres was behind the wheel of the Suburban and he was heading to her house. No one else lived down the lane but her.

She stood there, in the pale fall sun, uncertain of what to do, telling herself she didn't really want to see him. What did they have to say to each other that hadn't already been said? On the other hand, she was bored to tears and he could be a diversion.

She turned around to track the progress of the truck and within minutes, Andres appeared on her patio. She was the only person on the beach, and he spotted her instantly. Moving with his usual grace, he crossed the deck, then headed in her direction. Even as she told herself she shouldn't, she sat down on the sand to wait. Her eyes followed his approach, her heart suddenly thumping as she remembered Jeff's words the day he'd brought her home from the hospital. *Andres still cares about you.*

She'd given that pronouncement a lot of thought and she'd finally decided Jeff's interpretation was wrong. Andres's Latin pride had been hurt. He was staying to handle the Red Tide but not because he cared; he was going to deal with them because his macho sensibilities had been wounded. He'd been challenged and now he was going to take care of the situation. She and her injury were secondary to his motivation.

Jeff was definitely wrong.

"*Hola*, Lena. *¿Cómo estás?*" Andres pulled off his sunglasses as he reached her side, his voice smooth and low above the ocean's roar. Instead of his usual suit, he wore a pair of black slacks and a soft white sweater. The casual clothing made him look even sexier, and she responded to the pull, in spite of her best intentions. "How are you?" he repeated, this time in English.

"I'm doing fine," she said. "Just fine. No need to check up on me."

"I'm not checking up on you, Lena." Dropping to the sand, he sat down beside her. "I came to give you some news. I just talked to Bradley and he told me the FBI had prints of your shooter. His name was Esteban Olvera. He was a known Red Tide member. Not really active in public—which may mean something—but a clear connection all the same. His last known address was out of Miami."

"Miami!" Her mind went into overdrive. "Then he left a trail. He had to in order to get down here. A flight, a bus ride—something he might have paid for with a credit card. We can find out who paid him—"

"The P.D.'s already ahead of you. They think he might had driven over from the coast. They've found an abandoned car at the Silver Shore Motel. They're checking on it."

"That's great! They haven't pulled the vehicle

in yet, have they? We could stake it out and see—''

Andres held up one hand. "It's already been done, Lena. They have twenty-four hour surveillance on it."

"I want to call the captain. I need a copy of that report." She made an impatient gesture with her hand. "Do you have your phone on you—"

"Lena! It's being handled, all right?" He shook his head. "What's wrong? Don't you trust your department, either?"

"Of course I trust them! I just want to check on the situation, that's all." She stopped abruptly. "What do you mean...trust them, *either?*"

A gust of wind came off the surf and lifted his dark hair. He fingered it back above his brow. "Don't you remember your comment on the plane? I know how you feel about me, Lena."

She waited a second, her heart taking a jump at his unexpected words. Andres wasn't the kind of man who faced a problem head-on. He eased around it, finessed it, worked it smoothly. At least he had in the past.

She met his eyes. "You gave me good reason to feel that way."

Shocking her again, he agreed. "You're right, but perhaps you should tell your father as well as me. He seems to think I could convince you otherwise."

"I have told him," she said impatiently. "What makes him think that's changed—"

Andres waved off her question, a glint of gold catching the last rays of the dying sun. He wore a ring with a family crest on it. He'd told her once it was the only thing he'd brought from Havana, his grandfather's legacy. "I don't know why Phillip thinks the way he does, Lena. But he warned me to stay away from you. I told him you were old enough to take care of yourself, but I don't think he bought it."

Lena tightened her lips, her jaw going taut as she remembered the tension between the two men at the hospital. That's all she needed—Phillip and Andres fighting over what *she* should do with herself. She ignored the fact that Andres had actually defended her and made a mental note to call her father later and give him hell.

"Neither of you really have anything to say about it, but you both seem determined to tell me how to run my life. Why is that?"

He stayed silent for a moment, then Andres shifted in the sand and looked at her, his dark eyes unreadable for once. "Maybe you *need* some help. I know that's tough for you to accept, but it is possible, isn't it?"

"No," she answered hotly. "It isn't. I've been doing just fine without you. Your return, and your help, are the last things I want now. Two years ago things were different, but now..."

All at once, he seemed impatient with the subject. "Look, Lena, I know you're still angry at me for leaving you. I understand that completely. But believe this, I had no other choice, all right? As I told you back then, I *had* to do what I did. There simply wasn't any other option for me at the time."

She fought to cover up the hurt, but she didn't make it. Some of it slipped into her words, a bit more into her voice. He hadn't trusted her, professionally or personally, and the sting was still there. "I understand more than you think."

"No," he said bluntly. "You can't. It had nothing to do with you."

"Nothing to do—" Her mouth actually dropped open in amazement. "How on earth can you say it had nothing to do with me and keep a straight face? My God, Andres, do you really think I'm going to buy that?"

"You can take it or leave it, as you please," he said simply. "But it *is* the truth."

She scrambled awkwardly to her feet, her side protesting the movement with a quick stab of discomfort. Surprised by the force of it, she gasped and wobbled unexpectedly.

He stood instantly, his hands reaching out to steady her.

There was nothing she could do but accept his aid. If she refused, she'd fall down. She felt a moment's emotion as his stare, and his warm touch, registered. She didn't know what to call the feeling, but she knew one thing: she didn't want it.

"I'm telling you the truth," he repeated softly.

His voice held so much pain that she was suddenly flooded with the awful memory of the night he'd tried to explain. The look in his eyes, the anguish in his face, the hint of grief she'd thought later to have imagined. Had it all been real?

Of course not, she told herself immediately. If he'd felt that way, then why had he left?

She stepped back and spoke stiffly. "What happened back then is over and done with now."

"No. It will never be over, Lena. Not between us. It can't be."

Startled by his words, she looked up and into the dark well of his gaze. Once again she couldn't stop the deep longing, mixed with confusion and bewilderment, that came over her.

"Love doesn't die." The late sun lit his skin and painted it a deeper bronze. "It may change and take on different forms, but the emotions and feelings…they will always be there."

"Maybe for you—"

"For everyone," he countered before she could finish. "And if you were honest with yourself, you'd understand that and admit it." With his fingertip, he drew a heated line down the side of her jaw. His touch was gentle and her response frightening.

Averting her face, she looked out to the churning

water. The waves were as chaotic as her thoughts, but she revealed nothing other than coolness as she spoke. "You hurt me too much, Andres. You didn't trust me professionally and you destroyed me personally. I can't trust you again. It just wouldn't work."

"Trust is different from love."

She answered automatically, the words not really meaning anything to her anymore. "You can't have one without the other."

Turning her around until she was facing him, he stared at her until she was forced to meet his eyes. With a single finger he gently tapped a spot above her left breast. "This is where you love." Moving the finger to her head, he tapped again. "This is where trust comes from. They're two different things, *querida*. Very different. That's a lesson you should have learned by now."

SUNDAY MORNING Lena was more of a wreck than ever. She dialed Phillip several times to tell him to butt out of her life but he never answered, and finally she gave up and phoned his secretary of many years, Reba Dunn, at her condo. She told Lena he'd flown to Miami for a golf tournament and had yet to return. Reba usually went with Phillip on occasions like this, but she'd stayed home this time. A long-time divorcée, Reba liked her independence. She traveled often, her generous salary allowing her the best of all the exotic places.

Lena had always liked her, but Reba's news wasn't what she wanted to hear right now.

Unable to blow off steam by talking to her father, Lena spent the rest of the day doing everything she could to forget Saturday's conversation with Andres. Her constant busyness didn't do a thing but leave her exhausted.

ANDRES WASN'T THE MAN he used to be.

Walking into her office on Monday, Lena couldn't put her finger exactly on the change, but she understood a part of it. He was more direct, more to the point. Her realization only complicated things, and all the emotions she'd been fighting since he'd arrived surged forward. She cursed under her breath. She was still attracted to him, still felt the same old pull, and it was actually stronger than it had been before. Why, dammit? Why?

Everyone welcomed her back but before she could even sit down in her office, Bradley appeared in the doorway. "We just got a call," he announced. "I'm not too sure what's up yet but it's down on old 98. Destin P.D. has been on the scene a while and they can't seem to get things cleared up." He pivoted to leave. "I'll phone in as soon as I know what's going on—"

"No! Bradley, wait!" Lena moved from behind the desk, grateful for the interruption. A run was the only thing that would get her mind off Andres. "No phone calls. I'll come with you."

"Lena, please, this isn't necessary. You know what the doctor said—"

"Don't even try," she said briskly. "I'll stay in the War Wagon but I'm not spending the next six weeks sitting behind this desk. I can't."

He looked as if he wanted to argue.

"Forget it." Grabbing her jacket, she brushed past him and strode down the corridor. Sputtering at her pronouncement, Bradley ran to catch up. He didn't have another choice.

Thirty minutes later they reached the War Wagon, a remodeled Winnebago, parked two blocks from the small residential area near the beach. The camper contained an array of high-tech surveillance equipment plus the team's weapons, body armor and other major gear. Sarah manned the communications center anchored in the rear.

Sarah's fax machine was spitting out a document as Lena and Bradley entered the motor home. Bradley's size made the quarters feel even more cramped than they really were. He squirmed past the two women to take up a post near the front.

"What have we got?" Lena asked.

"It's the fourth house down." Sarah grabbed the fax and ripped it off the machine. "The tax rolls show that house is owned by a Robin Smith of Destin. We called and she said there were renters in it right now. A Mr. and Mrs. Paul Eliot."

"Mrs. Eliot's the one who made the initial call." Bradley stood at the front of the Winnebago. He was looking through the windshield with a pair of binoculars. The rest of the team was already in place at various locations around the house.

"Domestic disturbance?"

Nodding, Sarah answered, "Yes. She said he came in early this morning, they got into a fight, everything escalated. When he ran to the kitchen and grabbed a butcher knife, she fled to the neighbor's house and called the police. Now he's barricaded inside and won't come out. She's afraid he's going to harm himself."

Bradley offered Lena the glasses. She took them and scanned the area, but saw no movement inside or out.

"Is he alone?"

"As far as the P.D. knows, yes."

"Any weapons in the house besides the knife? Any guns?"

"The wife says no."

Lena handed the binoculars back to Bradley then turned to Sarah. "Get Mrs. Eliot on the phone." Slipping on her headset, she spoke quickly, locating all the team members Bradley had placed by phone on the way over—two men at the back of the house, two behind vehicles on the street, and the negotiator, Diego Sein. One of the two countersnipers available, Chase Mitchell, was working his way to the roof of a nearby church.

"Diego, have you talked to the guy yet?"

Lena's headset crackled as the negotiator spoke,

"No contact so far. We've called, but he won't answer the phone. I've tried the bullhorn, too, but got no response."

"Keep trying."

"Will do."

Sarah reached over Lena's shoulder and handed her the phone. "Here's Mrs. Eliot. She was talking to Diego, but she went back inside, to the house next door. We're keeping her out of sight for now."

Lena pulled away her headset and took the receiver. "Mrs. Eliot? This is Lieutenant Lena McKinney. I'm the commander of the SWAT team. What can you tell me about your husband that will help us resolve this situation?"

Mrs. Eliot's voice trembled so badly Lena could hardly understand her words. The longer they talked, the worse it got. Lena thanked her for her help and handed the phone back to Sarah a few seconds later. "That was pointless," she said. "The poor woman's a wreck. What do we know about this guy anyway?"

Hanging up the phone, Sarah handed her a second fax. The blurry photo and accompanying information weren't encouraging. A repeat offender, Mr. Eliot had just been released from the local county jail for his most recent DUI offense, one of many. Lena passed the sheet to Bradley. "Another fine citizen..."

A voice spoke in Lena's ear. It was Chase, the sniper. "I'm in place."

Lena put a hand to her microphone. "Copy that, C1."

She glanced at the house down the street. The tiny frame home looked well tended and neat. A new paint job gleamed in the sun and a row of oleanders waved along the sidewalk. Someone who lived in it cared. Mrs. Eliot, obviously. Thank God there weren't any children at home.

"Do we have the mirrors?" she asked.

Bradley nodded.

"Floor plan?"

"A rough sketch," Sarah answered.

Lena pulled her microphone to her lips and ordered one of the officers into the Wagon. A few minutes later, Brandon Friest rapped on the door and entered the Winnebago. He'd only been a team member for a few months, but Lena had been impressed with him so far. He was training to make front entries—a very dangerous position—and had been begging her to let him see some action. He tried to hide his anticipation as he waited for Lena to speak.

She tilted her head to where Sarah stood. "You've worked with these, right?"

Sarah held two of the devices she'd already pulled from the back of the supply cabinet. Reaching for them, the young officer nodded. Long and narrow, they were basically sticks with mirrors on the ends. "They're simple. No problem."

Lena tapped the penciled drawing on her desk. "The wife drew this and the owner confirmed it. If you can get to this back window, you'll have a straight shot from the den into the hallway. From what she said, he's probably in there."

He nodded without saying a word.

"You take the mirrors and approach the house the best way you can. Call in after you're positioned."

He turned and strode toward the door.

"Brandon?"

He stopped.

"Be careful."

She watched him leave the trailer and jog back into position. In a few minutes he disappeared behind the house. Five minutes after that he called in.

"I got 'em." His voice was excited now, pumped.

"What do you see?"

"The perp's pacing in the hallway. No weapon in sight."

"Are you positive?" Lena's heart thumped. "Look closely, Brandon. Be certain. The wife said he had a butcher knife."

"I don't see anything," he insisted. "I'm staring straight at his hands."

"Look everywhere."

After a second, he spoke again. "Nothing."

Lena nodded. "All right, then. Keep an eye on him."

Two hours later they still had no movement. Diego had talked until he was hoarse and the man inside had yet to say a word. He continued to pace the hallway with almost manic concentration. His wife denied the possibility, but he had to be on drugs, probably meth.

They waited another hour and Lena knew she didn't have much more time. Three to four hours was the limit with one team. She'd have to switch men, a tricky operation at best, or move in. With the information they had, going forward seemed safe, a nonlethal solution that would work out best for everyone. She checked with Brandon one more time. He assured her he saw no weapons, no guns, no bombs, no anything.

Pulling her microphone closer, Lena outlined the plan, a standard one for entry in a situation without weapons. A few minutes later, from her seat in the Winnebago, she watched the surreptitious movements of her men as they took their places. Brandon continued to monitor the suspect with his mirrors as another officer assembled the battering ram and a third one prepared the tear gas. Lena took a deep breath, then she gave the go-ahead and the team swarmed inside the little house, disappearing through the doorway.

No one was ready for what happened next.

CHAPTER SEVEN

THE SOUND OF gunfire echoed through the neighbourhood, and pandemonium immediately erupted. Lena watched in horror then she and Bradley turned in unison and rushed to the exit of the Winnebago. She yelled instructions to Sarah as they tumbled out. "Get the standby ambulance out here now. And call for backup black and whites! Hurry!"

By the time they reached the front porch, it was over. A man she didn't recognize was on his back in the hallway, bleeding from a shoulder wound. His weapon, a .22 caliber pistol, was twirling in a nearby corner, obviously sent there by someone's boot. Lena's gaze caught the movement, then skipped over it to the opening to the living room. Another man lay there. He was stretched out, his arms flung to the sides. It was Brandon.

She ran to the young cop's side and kneeled beside him. "Brandon! Brandon! Can you hear me?"

He didn't respond. With her pulse roaring, Lena let her eyes go over his body, her hands following their path. She could see no blood, find no injury.

After a heart-stopping second, his eyes fluttered open. "I—I'm o-okay," he stuttered. "I took a hit but my vest caught it. I—I can't breathe."

Relief washed over Lena, leaving her weak. She sat down abruptly on the scuffed wooden floor.

Bradley bent over the other man. "This one's alive," he pronounced. "He'll make it." As he spoke, he glanced toward Lena, his expression suddenly alarmed. "You okay?"

Lena nodded. Her side was screaming and her head spinning, but neither complaint meant anything. All she could think about was how close to disaster the team had come. Another inch and she'd be talking to the widow of the officer lying beside her. They'd never lost a member—not like this—and she didn't intend for it to ever happen, either. Not on her watch. Closing her eyes, Lena fought the nausea that was threatening her now that she knew everyone was all right. She opened her eyes a second later and looked down at Brandon.

"What happened?" She wanted to shriek the question, but her voice was calm. "I thought you gave it the all clear. You said he didn't have any weapons."

"I—I thought so, too. I—I swear to God, Lena. I don't know where the gun came from...."

Patting his shoulder, she watched him struggle—to catch his breath and to accept what had almost happened. "It's okay, Brandon. I shouldn't have let you do this on your own."

Looking down at the flushed, scared face of the young officer, Lena tried to smile reassuringly. She wasn't lying. She should *never* have given him total responsibility. She should have let one of the more experienced men supervise him. Hell, she should have gone outside *herself* and double-checked.

He'd almost died, and it was no one's fault but hers.

ANDRES LEFT his office after work that evening and headed downtown to the SWAT team's offices. On the seat of the Suburban was the report from Washington on Esteban Olvera. Andres could have e-mailed it, he could have faxed it, he could have even sent Carmen over with the papers, but none of those options had appealed to him, and he knew why.

He wanted to see Lena.

Their conversation at the beach had left him dissatisfied. There was too much unfinished business between them, and though he knew it had to stay that way, he didn't like it. Maybe there was something he could say...

The drive didn't take ten minutes. Parking the SUV in the evening dusk, he entered the squat, concrete building. He'd been to the SWAT headquarters several times since arriving, talking to Bradley and making the various arrangements he'd needed for his own office, but the appearance of the place never improved. It looked and smelled like every government building he'd ever worked in. Bare and institutional, the station was located within minutes of some of the most expensive real estate in Florida, but no one would ever know that just from looking at it.

Andres passed a warren of cubicles before he got close to Lena's office. The area was deserted with not a soul in sight, but just as he'd expected, Lena was still there. He could hear her voice as he neared the back, and he knew instantly something was wrong. He increased his pace and rounded the corner quickly.

She was perched on the edge of her desk, a pained expression on her face as she spoke over the phone. Her windblown hair and disheveled appearance did nothing to lessen her appeal, but it did tell him one thing; she'd been on a call. Not sitting in her chair taking it easy, writing reports or reading training materials.

She'd been out.

His first response was anger. What in the hell did she think she was doing? Didn't she know she had to take care of herself? She hadn't healed yet, dammit. But when he heard her words, his irritation turned into concern.

"He'll be okay?" she asked. "Just bruises, then, no broken ribs or anything?" She nodded to herself. "Good, good...and the perp?"

She looked up at that point, as if sensing Andres's presence. Her gray gaze widened, and she beckoned him inside. Her motion seemed to hold reluctance, but he didn't care.

She listened a bit more and said, "All right. Thanks for the update. Please keep us informed." She hung up the phone and looked at him.

"What's wrong?"

She started to answer him, then stopped. Obviously upset and angry, she blinked furiously and turned away from him to stare up at the ceiling, cursing all the while. He crossed the office and pulled her around so he could look at her. Her gaze was tumultuous as she continued to fight her emotions, clearly hating the fact that he was a witness to them.

"¿Qué tal, mi amor? ¿Qué pasa?"

After a few moments, she tried to step away from him again but he wouldn't let her go.

"What's wrong? What happened?"

"We had a run." She looked shaky, not quite together. "It didn't go well."

"Was anyone hurt?"

"Yes. But not seriously."

He lifted a thumb and feathered it over her cheek. "Then what's the problem? This isn't like you, no?"

"I screwed up, Andres." She shook her head in a measure of misery. "Someone could have really been hurt, maybe even killed. I sent the men in when I shouldn't have." She gave him the details in a halting way. When she finished, she shook her head. "First the airport, now this... I think I might be losing it. Really losing it."

He waited a beat, then spoke harshly. "Don't be stupid, Lena!"

She jerked her gaze to his. She'd expected sympathy, words of compassion, and he'd given her this. It threw her off guard and that was exactly why he'd said it.

"Everyone makes mistakes. Remember what you said at the airport? *I'm not perfect... and neither are my men.*' Those were your exact words. Have you forgotten so soon?"

"But I shouldn't have—"

He raised his palm again. "Are you listening to me? You. Aren't. Perfect. And neither is your team. Mistakes get made all the time. And many end up with worse outcomes than this." His eyes narrowed. "Trust me on this, Lena. You won't ever forget it, but it doesn't mean you can't do your job anymore."

He could tell his words reached her. It was a risk, but he'd had to take it to make her feel better. She took a deep breath and blinked twice, making the connection he'd known she would.

"This—this has happened to you?"

"Something like it." He paused. "Only much worse. I lost a man. It wasn't my fault, but I felt responsible."

"I had no idea."

"I did the best I could, but my best wasn't good enough. Someone else was ahead of me in the game and my man was killed. He wasn't simply an officer, either. He was my best friend."

"Oh, God, Andres. How awful! I didn't know...."

"You couldn't have known. It wasn't something you would have read about in the papers. I'm only telling you about it now to help you."

"Did you get the shooter?"

They were reaching thin ice, but he had to answer her questions. It would seem strange if he didn't. "No, I didn't catch him. For several months I investigated the man I felt was responsible—the man who paid to make sure it happened—but I found no proof. I had to let it go."

This time it was her voice that turned soft, the words a whisper between them. "You must have been devastated."

He looked up and noticed, for the first time, the tiny lines radiating from the corners of her eyes. Lines that hadn't been there before. Lines *he'd* put there. He reached out and touched them gently.

"I suffered another loss about the same time," he said. "I didn't know which one to mourn the most so I grieved for neither. It seemed best."

Her lips were fuller than they had been, he thought to himself, somehow more lush. Strands of her hair, a jumbled-up mess, gleamed under the lights. The silent, deserted office suddenly made it seem as if they were the last two people on earth, and Andres went still. No words were exchanged to break the quiet, but they continued to communicate. Her pain, his guilt. His regret, her anger. It flowed between them in a river of feelings and emotions.

Their lips met a moment later.

It seemed odd, he thought, how perfectly they fit together, how closely matched they were. She nestled under his arms and against his chest as if they truly were two halves of one whole. At the same time, her curves had changed since they'd been apart. Her body was harder, leaner, the muscles beneath his hands as tight and well-formed as his own, her strength more sensual and erotic than the softness of the other women he'd known.

Andres's desire took another leap as she opened her mouth to his. *This* was what it'd been like, he thought. *This* was what had always been between them. Their passion had been a thing alive, an entity they almost couldn't control.

In the back of his mind, Andres knew he should stop. This was a mistake. For one thing, they were in her office. They'd done rasher things when they'd been together before, but this was different…or it should have been.

More importantly, though, Lena was upset and seeking something that would erase the pain, something that would make her forget. She didn't love him as she once had and she never would again. He'd hurt her too deeply to ever hope for that.

His body didn't seem to care.

The heat between them only increased, her hands drawing him to her, a friction building between them that would quickly become impossible to control. He would have chastised himself for the rush, but it was obvious Lena felt the same way. Her kiss deepened and so did the moan in the back of her throat. Despite her words to the contrary it was clear she wanted him as much as he wanted her. Maybe that was why she'd pushed him away so much. If Lena did need him—for anything— nothing would be more scary to her, would it?

He didn't have time to think about the implication of the revelation.

The door to her office flew open unexpectedly. With a guilty start, they jumped away as if they were two teenagers caught necking on the front porch. Her T-shirt was halfway up her chest, and Lena scrambled to pull the black fabric down. She glanced at Andres. He ran a hand over his crooked tie and tried not to look too dazed.

Beck Winters stood on the threshold, his ice blue eyes wide open with surprise. He immediately began to back out of the room. "I'm sorry."

His resounding voice rumbled down the hallway and Lena flinched. It was bad enough that he'd seen. Did he have to alert everyone else, too? It was late, yes, but who knew who was listening?

"I didn't mean to interrupt. Why don't I come back later—"

"Beck—it—it's okay. Really…" Her words said one thing while her mind screamed another. Like hell, it was okay! What did she think she was doing? Had she totally lost her mind? She should have never let Andres into her office when she'd been so distressed. "Wh-what did you need?"

Beck threw a glance at Andres but said nothing. Instead, they exchanged some kind of silent message. She sharpened her voice and spoke again. "What did you want, Beck?"

His eyes came back to hers. "I was wondering if you'd heard from the hospital," he said calmly. "About Brandon."

"He's fine." She gave him the details. "I'd appreciate it if you'd pass the information on to everyone," she said briskly. "And tell them also we'll have a special debriefing tomorrow. At 4:00 p.m. sharp."

He nodded then gave Andres another look and stepped outside the office, closing the door behind him with a snap.

Lena counted to three, then she faced Andres. "I think you need to leave."

"Lena…"

"No." She shook her head. "Don't say anything. Just go."

His black eyes went darker then he drew his

mouth into a narrow line. Without a word, he went out the door.

LENA SAT ON THE DECK that evening after her workout and watched the sun go down. It was a huge ball of orange and red and it lit the sky for miles, turning the water beneath to fire. The weather had changed again, and it was cold. She'd worn an extra sweatshirt for her walk, but in reality, the temperature had nothing to do with the chill she was feeling.

She was scared. Scared to death.

Half the feeling came from the call-out. Things could have so easily gone the other way. Brandon could have been killed. The shooter might have died. Civilians could have been wounded. It was only through God's grace that they hadn't suffered more casualties. If the suspect had had a better weapon, the damage could have been tragic.

She should have been more careful. The two most dangerous times during a call-out were at the beginning and at the end. If the setup wasn't perfect, the team could be spotted, leaving them vulnerable. And if the takedown wasn't done properly, it was just as dangerous.

Hostage takers regularly committed suicide by cop. Too frightened to kill themselves, often they'd "surrender" then raise their weapons and step into the resulting line of fire. Let a cop take the responsibility. Lena had seen more than one officer devastated by that outcome.

It was her job to see that didn't happen. She had to protect the citizens of Destin *and* her men. They depended on her to do the right thing. And she wasn't sure she could anymore. The incident at the airport and now this had left her shaken and unsure of herself. If she'd been concentrating on work instead of Andres, neither situation would have happened.

Andres. The source of all her problems.

She stewed about him for a while then accepted reality. She *wanted* to blame him for everything, but inside her heart, she knew he wasn't her problem. She was.

She'd been thinking about him long before the call-out. He'd occupied her brain ever since he'd stepped off that jet. When he'd come into her office, he'd come at the worst possible time, too. She'd wanted his warm embrace, and his revelation had made her feel better. She was falling into his trap.

Blinking into the dying light, she thought of the other truth he'd told her, not with words, but by the way his mouth had felt and how his arms had molded around her body. He'd wanted her, just as she'd wanted him.

She shook her head and shivered, confusion filling her thoughts with chaos. The sexual spark was still there, but did that erase all the hurt, all the pain, that had come later?

The phone suddenly sounded inside the house, shattering her thoughts. Jumping up, Lena ran through the door and caught it on the fourth ring. Phillip's sonorous voice answered her breathy hello.

"Reba told me you called yesterday. She said you sounded upset. How are you feeling? Do you need anything?"

"Actually, I do need something." Tired and angry, she didn't bother to hide her frustration. "I need you to keep your nose out of my business. Andres told me about the conversation you two had last week, and frankly I didn't appreciate it."

Her father didn't say anything for a moment. "He told you about it? All of it?"

His words held a hint of unease, which surprised her. It wasn't his usual style. Maybe he understood, for once, that she could handle this one on her own. And maybe she was indulging in wishful thinking.

"He told me enough," she answered. "Dad, I don't need your help with this. I resent you talking to Andres about it, too. I'm a grown woman—"

He interrupted. "He's not good enough for you—"

"Stop right there."

He fell silent, and she continued. "You don't

have to give me reasons to stay away from him, okay? I have enough of them already.''

''I was only trying to help.''

''No, you were trying to do what you usually do. Manipulate and control. But in this case, you don't have to worry. I'm not interested in Andres and I've told him that.'' She looked out the window. Night had come over the beach and all she could see was darkness. It reminded her of Andres's gaze and the way she'd felt when they'd kissed. She closed her eyes and shut out the view...and the memory. ''He knows how I feel. And there's nothing else to say about it. Your help isn't necessary.''

They spoke a few more minutes, then Phillip rang off. Lena threw a frozen dinner into the microwave and tried to blank her mind. One thing keep intruding, and surprisingly, it wasn't Andres or the call-out. It was the hesitant way her father had spoken when she'd told him she knew of his conversation with Andres. His reluctance was very unusual, and the more she thought about it, the more she wondered what had caused it.

''I'VE POSTED the schedule outside.'' Winding up their usual Tuesday staff meeting, Lena spoke briskly even though she felt like hell. She was anxious and still reeling from the encounter with Andres. ''I know Thanksgiving is coming up and I tried to give the family men first consideration, but even so, most of you will need to stay in town. I'm sorry I couldn't do better. If you have a problem with the roster, please come see me. Any questions?''

When no one spoke, she gathered up her notes. ''All right, then, if that's it, we're finished.'' The sound of scraping chairs and low conversation took over. Relieved the long day had come to an end, Lena headed for the back of the conference room. Beck stopped her as she reached the door.

She'd managed to avoid him up to this point and had been hoping for a clean escape. It wasn't going to happen.

''I'd like to talk to you, Lieutenant. Do you have the time?''

She wanted to lie, but she couldn't. This was Beck. If the team was her second family, Beck was her closest brother. She waited a beat, then answered with a sigh. ''C'mon back to my office.''

He closed the door behind him as she rounded her desk and pulled out her chair.

''What are you doing?'' he said quietly.

''I'm sitting down—''

''That's not what I mean and you know it.'' He waved a hand toward the corner. ''I'm talking about what I saw in here yesterday. I've tried to figure it out and I can't.'' He shook his head. ''You and Andres? What's going on, Lena?''

She met his bright, blue eyes, but said nothing.

''You were kissing him.''

"No. He was kissing me."

"Right." A skeptical expression came over his features. "It certainly looked to me as if there was mutual participation going on."

"Well, what if there was?" she asked, suddenly defensive. "Would that be so awful?"

"I don't think so. I always liked Andres, but you're the one who said he'd never darken your doorstep again. I'd hate to see you get hurt as badly as you were before." He crossed his arms and waited.

She shook her head, unable to answer. Swinging her chair around, she fought the urge to remember, but her body took her back. The heat of him against her and the warmth of his mouth… God, how long had it been since she'd felt truly loved by a man? Too long. Way too long.

But he didn't love her.

Abruptly, she swung the chair back. "It was nothing. He came in here right after the Eliot situation, and I was upset. He was trying to make me feel better and it got out of hand. End of story."

Beck sat down in the chair in front of her desk and linked his hands over his chest. He stared at her and said nothing.

Finally, she spoke. "That was it, okay?"

"If that was it, then why are you so defensive?"

"I'm defensive because you're sitting there grilling me. Anyone would be."

He shook his head, his blond hair gleaming under the harsh lights of her office. "Are you falling for him again?"

"No! Absolutely not! That's crazy," she answered quickly. "I'm not falling for Andres, okay? He walked out on me. I wouldn't give him another chance if he was the last man on earth. My father hates him, he hurt me, there's too much bad history between us—"

"I don't need the list, Lena. I've heard it before."

"Then why are you in here, giving me a hard time?"

"I'm not giving you a hard time. I came in here because I thought you might want to talk about what's happening. I'm trying to be your friend." His blue eyes seemed to glow as he leaned toward her. "Let's be honest, Lena. In the feelings department, you aren't always on top of things, mainly because you don't want to be."

There was nothing she could say. He knew her too well. He stared at her and she stared back.

Finally, Beck broke the silence. "Lena— c'mon...if you *didn't* still have feelings for him, we wouldn't be having this conversation. You wouldn't care. Is it your father? Are you afraid of what he'd say—"

"Dad has nothing to do with this."

"Then what?"

She stood up and crossed her office to stand beside the window. "I can't care about Andres," she said softly. "I can't let myself."

"Why not? He obviously cares—"

She pivoted. "Beck, he doesn't give a damn about me, okay? He kissed me because he could. I let him. I wanted him to do it. I felt like shit and I needed to feel better any way I could." She paused to gather her thoughts. They refused to be corralled, though, and all she could do was be blunt. "The truth of the matter is that Andres doesn't love me...and I *can't* love him. It would hurt too much to go through all that again. And I don't intend to do it." She stopped, then spoke again a second later. "I *won't* do it again."

CHAPTER EIGHT

WHEN HE'D DECIDED to stay in Destin, Andres had told Carmen to rent a condo for him. He hadn't seen the unit at Oceania until the night she'd called and told him it was his. He'd moved into the furnished place right then and there. Stretching along the beach in an area known as Holiday Isle, the pristine white building was steps away from the frothy emerald water. It was a setting straight out of paradise.

But wasted on him. He rarely came home before nine or ten. Opening the office had turned out to be more complicated than he'd anticipated. And that wasn't the only thing he'd misjudged, either.

Coming home Tuesday night, he thought of the encounter he'd shared with Lena the week before. Truth be told, he'd thought of little else since it'd happened, and with every passing moment his irritation had only grown. The kiss had left him wanting more, but it clearly hadn't had the same effect on her. Tossing him out of her office had made *that* point obvious. All he'd wanted to do was make her feel better, to help her with her problem, and that was the thanks he'd gotten. He should have known better. She couldn't accept help from anyone. Not even when she needed it. Not even when she *asked* for it.

He threw his coat and briefcase to a nearby chair and strode to the wet bar in one corner of the den. Carmen had stocked it well, and he pulled a beer from the under-counter refrigerator and popped it open.

He searched his brain for something other than Lena to occupy it, and in two quick strides, he went back to the chair and snapped open his attaché. Maybe the report he'd just picked up would capture his attention. It'd come in late that afternoon, a detailed account of the surveillance being conducted on the car abandoned at the Silver Shore Motel. As soon as Andres had known he was staying in Destin, he'd informed the different agencies involved and asked for copies of their weekly status updates.

He skimmed over the written summaries then skipped down to the bottom of the page. He had to give the local P.D. credit—they were certainly thorough. Each shift had noted every car model, make and license that had passed through the parking lot. Thankfully it was a small motel. According to Bradley, it had a reputation for being the local hot-sheet place, but prostitution wasn't a high priority in the area. Most of the renters were fishermen who didn't want better or retirees who couldn't afford nicer. There were only a dozen units, each a tiny bungalow. A strip of parking spots lined one side making it easy to see who came and went.

He flipped to the back of the folder, past the list of cars. A contact sheet of photographs had also been included. A date at the bottom of the first one told him the pictures had all been taken the day after the watch had begun. There were two more sheets for the two subsequent days, then just the listings. Andres glanced at them then dropped the papers on the nearby coffee table. He'd have Carmen run a check on the Dade County tags tomorrow. She'd been surly lately, which meant she'd point out the uselessness of the effort, but in the end, she'd do it. What else *could* they do?

Taking his drink, Andres wandered into the kitchen and opened the freezer. It was supplied as well as the bar. Frozen dinners. Gourmet meals. Anything he could ask for from soup to steaks. With his beer in his hand, he stood beside the door, the cold air whispering over him. He wasn't hungry. He wasn't thirsty. And he sure as hell didn't want to work.

He didn't want anything...but Lena. The feel of her in his arms was suddenly so real, so immediate, his body responded as if she were right in front of him. She'd thrown him out, yes, but she'd kissed him first. And Lena didn't do anything lightly. The encounter had to have meant something to her, too.

Shoving the freezer door closed with a crash, he reeled around to stare out the nearby wall of windows, a cloud of condensation wisping up to the ceiling as he eyed the dark and empty beach. For a few tortured minutes, he wrestled with himself, then muttering a Spanish curse, he gave up.

Slamming the still-full can of beer to the counter, he grabbed his car keys and left.

HER DOORBELL rang at ten.

Startled, Lena looked up from the news she hadn't been watching. She'd come home at eight and had a glass of wine with a piece of leftover pizza. With Bradley on call, she'd decided to have another glass as well. Because of her twenty-four hour status, she hardly ever drank, but it'd been a helluva week so far and it was only Tuesday. She figured she deserved to unwind, and alcohol was the only way she'd manage it. Without the liquid therapy, her mind would continue to spin.

The bell sounded again and she jumped up from the couch. Grabbing her service revolver from the locked drawer beside her bed, she returned to the entry, the weapon tucked into the curve of her back, beneath the loose waistband of her sweatpants. With one hand on the pistol's grip, she flipped on the porch light—and stared in surprise.

Andres waited under the bare bulb. He looked irritated and out of sorts...and sexy beyond belief, his shirt crinkled and unbuttoned at the neck, his

jacket hooked over his shoulder with one crooked
finger. The shadow of his beard told her he hadn't
shaved since morning and the turbulence in his
eyes told her she was in for a rough time.

With unsteady hands, she threw the dead bolt
and opened the door. He stood without moving and
didn't say a word. Her heart began to thud with an
out-of-sync rhythm, and all she wanted to do was
pull him inside and throw herself at him.

But she didn't.

Blocking the door with her body, she spoke
calmly and rationally. "Andres! What a surprise.
Did you need something?"

"Lena." He said her name formally. His gaze
was tempestuous, his words heavy with a Spanish
lilt. "I want to talk to you, and I don't intend to
do it out here."

She hesitated for a fleeting second, then told herself she had no other option. Operating out of
habit, she threw the locks behind him after he
stepped inside and flipped off the light as well,
removing her gun to lay it on the table by the door
where he'd already dropped his coat. The hallway
was narrow and dark, and when she turned, he was
right behind her.

He spoke bluntly and without any warning. "We
have some unfinished business." Raising his arms,
he placed his hands on either side of her head,
trapping her between the wall and the door.

They weren't touching, but she could feel the

heat rising off his body. A tremor of desire shimmered down her spine and into her legs, leaving her with the wish that she'd never opened the door.

"Unfinished business?" she repeated. "What would that be?"

"You know what I'm talking about. I'm here to complete the conversation we started in your office. The one that got interrupted."

"That wasn't a conversation." She licked her lips. "A conversation uses words."

She could barely see his expression, but it didn't matter. His voice—and his body—were communicating everything she needed to know.

"You used words," he said quietly. "But they didn't match what you did. We need to clear up that contradiction. Right now. Right here."

All she could think of was what Beck had said and suddenly she didn't know how to answer because Andres had told the truth. Her body felt one way but her mind felt another. And her heart? She had no idea in hell what it felt.

Without replying, she ducked underneath his arm and started down the hallway, but he grabbed her before she managed two steps. She stopped instantly, but he didn't release her.

"I want to talk about us." His fingers—those long, slim fingers she'd always loved so much—tightened on her arm. It seemed as if they were around her heart, too, squeezing just as hard. She let her eyes land on his and he spoke again. "Let's get it out once and for all, and end this charade. It's way overdue.''

HER GRAY EYES darkened as his words penetrated. He was pushing her, and pushing Lena was not a smart thing to do. He didn't care, though; he had to know.

"I've told you how I feel," she said hotly. "I've made it more than clear. There's nothing else to say."

"Then which was a lie?" He made his voice soft and deliberate. "Your words…or your kiss?"

"I didn't lie to you. I don't lie to anyone."

He paused a second. "Not even to yourself?"

She stared at him, and in the tension-filled silence, Andres moved closer to her. She never wore perfume, a necessity of her job, but he could smell the scent of her skin. He knew it as well as his own. Even if he had wanted to resist, he couldn't have; like an expensive fragrance, it drew him in.

She parted her lips as if to say something, but he didn't give her the chance. He lowered his head, his mouth covering hers with an urgency neither could deny. If she shoved him aside or told him to quit, he'd leave at her command. It was her choice and she knew it, but he needed an answer, one way or the other.

She didn't stop him.

The only thing either of them cared about was the embrace and experiencing everything that went with the physical part of their relationship. *Everything*.

Kissing her passionately, he moved his hands up her arms and gripped her shoulders tightly. Then she groaned his name into his mouth, and that was all it took.

Andres backed her against the wall and pulled at her sweater. Without a murmur, she lifted her arms and let him tug it off, her fingers fumbling with the buttons on his shirt the minute her own garment fell at their feet. He helped her as much as he could, then he simply gave up and tore it off. A button pinged against the tile floor.

"Oh, Lena...*querida*..." He whispered her name as he buried his face in the sweet juncture between her shoulder and her neck. Her warmth was like velvet beneath his mouth, so soft and sensual he couldn't believe it. Had she always been like this? Had he known her secrets before and ignored them or had he simply put them from his mind realizing he could no longer experience them after he'd left?

Either way, he didn't care. What mattered now was only the moment. He nipped at her skin with his teeth, making his way up her neck with tiny bites of pleasure. She whimpered and spread her hands against his chest, threading her fingers in his dense, black hair. For a moment, they stayed that way. Then she moved again, her hands going lower to the zipper of his pants.

He didn't wait. He couldn't. Andres pulled her toward him, his lips against her breasts. She wore a white cotton bra, no lace or frills, and it was the sexiest piece of lingerie he'd ever seen on a woman. Slipping his hand behind her back, he undid the clasp and the garment fluttered to the floor. He covered her breasts with his fingers. They were as perfect as he remembered. Taut and small, and peaked with desire. Licking her nipples with his tongue, he spread his hands against the satin of her back then began to tug at her slacks.

In another minute, they came off and she stood before him—almost nude. Her white panties gleamed in the darkness and unlike her bra, they were silk. And transparent. Dropping to his knees, he leaned toward her and kissed her through them, then he opened his mouth and pressed his tongue to the fabric. She groaned as he went lower.

When they slid to the floor, she landed on top.

THEY MOVED to her bedroom an hour later. Andres carried her through the darkened house to the bed and placed her gently on the comforter. Their lovemaking resumed, but it took on a different quality. Slower, almost dreamlike now, he touched her gently, his warm hands and long fingers trailing over her face and limbs as if he were renewing memories too long repressed. She reveled in his touch and wondered how she'd lived the past two years without it.

She knew the answer. She hadn't lived; she'd been in a deep freeze with no emotions getting in and nothing leaving, either. She'd gone through the motions and finally convinced herself that what she was doing *was* living, but inside, as she'd known all along, she was fooling herself.

He stroked her stomach, his fingers brushing lower. *This,* she thought, was living. A man's touch warming her, his breath against her skin. Everything else was a sham.

Some time passed before he made his way back up her body and kissed her lips again. "You're so beautiful," he whispered. "So perfect. You make me homesick, *querida*...."

She reached out and put her hand against his jaw. His stubble was almost soft. "What do you mean? Homesick?"

Covering her fingers with his own, he shook his head. "I'm not sure I can explain *la isla*...."

Her heart swelled. When they'd been together before, he'd never talked about the island he'd left. She hadn't pressed, either. It was too painful for him, she'd always assumed. "Is it hard to talk about it?" she asked now.

"Sometimes, yes. But lying here with you, I'm reminded of the beaches, the long hot days, the laughter...everything good that I abandoned and can never get back." His eyes went to hers. "You would have liked *mi familia*. And they would have loved you."

She eased up on one elbow and looked at him. She knew so little. "Tell me about them."

"My parents were poor. They both worked hard, long hours. My mother was a day laborer at one of the big family *fincas*—farms—outside of town. My father fished. My only other relative was Tia Isabel."

Lena had met his aunt. Isabel Gaspar was still a beauty—elegant and long-limbed with transparent skin, silver hair and piercing, black eyes. Andres had paid a fortune to bring her out of the country and into America.

"Does she still live in Miami?"

He nodded. "I bought her a new condo in a nice high-rise building a few years ago. The stairs in the town house were getting to her, and I wanted to see her somewhere safer."

Lena dredged up other tiny bits he'd told her before. "You didn't have any brothers or sisters, right?"

"That's right. I asked my mother once why not. I knew she went to the *santera* a lot and bought candles to light. I heard her praying at night while my father was gone on his boat."

"The *santera?*"

"A kind of priest," he explained. "A lot of Cubans believe in Santería. It's a mixture of African religion and Catholicism. A *santera* helps you with everything, from getting pregnant to making someone fall in love with you."

"What did your mother say?"

"She started to cry. I never asked again."

Lena thought of her own four brothers then. "You didn't miss much," she said dryly.

"Maybe so," he answered, "but in Cuba, it's different. The larger the family, the more people to work. When my father was sent to prison, we could have used the extra hands."

"Your father was arrested?" She looked at him in surprise. "For what?"

"Arrested?" He shook his head wearily. "That implies justice, a trial, some kind of fairness. That's not how it works down there, Lena. They came to the house and took him away to *La Cabaña*. He was a political prisoner for almost ten years."

"So they released him?"

"No. He passed away in prison—which is unusual. Generally they let them out to die. They say the only way to escape La Cabaña is to go with the devil. It's almost a joke in Havana."

"It might be a joke but it isn't a funny one."

"No, it's not, you're right. There are three or four hundred political prisoners, as we speak, rotting in jails over there. For no good reason."

His eyes held so much pain, she felt the pangs herself. Reaching out, she pulled him closer to her. He'd never shared this with her before, never given her the heartbreaking details. She didn't know what to do except comfort him.

Accepting her embrace, he sought her solace, but in a different manner. He was a man, and for him there was only one way to face the long-ago hurts. Reaching out—once more—for the condoms he'd placed on the nightstand, Andres wrapped his arms around her and rolled them both to the center of the bed where he began to kiss her all over again. Swept into his arms and into his anguish as well, Lena let him do what he did best.

FOR A MOMENT, Andres didn't know where he was when he woke up, then everything registered. Lena's motionless form sleeping beside him, the scent of their lovemaking still in the air, the quiet ticking of her bedside clock. He glanced toward the luminous dial and read the glowing green numerals—3:00 a.m.

Slipping his arm from beneath her bare shoulders, he eased away and climbed out of the bed. When they'd been together before Lena had always insisted he go after they make love. She didn't want him to spend the night. Not before they were married, she'd said. It'd irritated him, but at the same time it was a quirk he'd found endearing.

As he looked down at her now, she murmured and shifted in the bed but she didn't wake up, the sheet falling to her waist at her movement. Her hair was a silken sheen against the pillowcase, the still-healing line of her scar a shadow against her paler skin. He reached out but stopped just short of touching it.

What had he done by coming here tonight?

Turning away from the bed and from his question, Andres went back to the entry and the pile of abandoned clothing. It was cold in the quiet, still house. He slipped on his pants and then thrust his arms into his shirt but he didn't bother to do it up; he couldn't have anyway. Half the buttons were gone.

He returned to the living room and was almost to the bedroom when he heard a clicking noise. It was coming from one of the huge windows off the deck on the rear of the old house. Immediately curious, he crossed the room and spotted the source of the sound. Lena had a row of pots sitting out on the covered deck, and each one held a single rosebush. The plant nearest the window was tapping the glass with its leaves, almost as if it wanted inside. His eyes, now adjusted to the dark, caught the subtle sway of the rest of the plant. It was covered in pale-pink blossoms, some open, some still closed. How she'd managed to get the rose to bloom at this time of year, he didn't know, but it seemed to be fate.

He opened the window and plucked the nearest flower. Going back into the bedroom, he laid the bloom on the pillow beside Lena's head, then kissing her softly, he turned and left.

LENA HEARD the front door shut and sat up in bed. As she moved, she jostled the pillow beside her and the flower Andres had left tumbled into the knotted sheets. She picked it up and brought it to her nose. Above the blossom's fragrance she caught a salty hint of the ocean and the lingering scent of his aftershave.

She'd awakened the minute he'd left the bed, but she'd kept her eyes closed, feigning sleep. She didn't know what to say to him or how to act; it'd seemed simpler to pretend she was still asleep. She heard him start his car, then she listened to the whine of the motor as he turned around in the driveway and headed away from the house.

She fell back into the wrinkled sheets and threw an arm over her eyes. She couldn't block the images, though. His body, his mouth, his hands… every last detail she'd spent the past two years trying to forget was now so fresh she could still feel them on her skin. Now there was something new to add to the mental scrapbook: his memories of his home. He'd shared his body with her before, but never his past. They seemed tied together even more closely than they had been before.

Why on earth had she unlocked that door?

CHAPTER NINE

ANDRES HAD ALREADY called twice by the time Lena made it into the office the next morning. She stood beside her desk and fingered the pink telephone slips, pondering what to do. She didn't want to call him back because she couldn't tell him everything she was feeling. His touch had affected her even more than it used to; she was reeling from the emotions that had taken place between them. Their relationship had always been a powerful one, but last night had gone beyond even that.

She knew only one thing for certain. They couldn't repeat what had happened. Not until she had things sorted out.

Her ringing phone saved her. Dropping the messages, she picked up the receiver, listened to Bradley's news of a call-out, then raced out into the hallway, grateful for the interruption. Fifteen minutes later, she was in a squad car heading due west toward Fort Walton with Bradley at the wheel.

A small community between Pensacola and Destin, Fort Walton had its share of SWAT calls. Most of the military people from Eglin Air Force Base lived within its confines or nearby, and the soldiers had the same problems a lot of young men did— too much energy and not enough money. They were highly trained and highly stressed and things sometimes got tense.

But this wasn't to be one of those times. Lena's cell phone rang before they could get on-site.

"Turn around," Sarah said calmly. "Everything's over."

Lena put a hand over her phone and looked at Bradley. "It's Sarah. She says to forget about it."

He raised his eyebrows and slowed the car.

"What happened?" Lena asked.

"It was a fugitive arrest, a parolee. The parole office hadn't seen him in about three months and they finally tracked him down. They thought there was going to be trouble, but the guy came out when his mother happened to show up. They took him down and everything's fine. The Fort Walton people will wrap it up."

Hanging up the phone, Lena explained and Bradley headed back to the office. The aborted call was a harbinger of what was to come. Missing reports, a canceled court appearance, two men out with the flu… Lena was exhausted by the time she finished the paperwork that had piled up on her desk and was shocked to discover it was 7:00 p.m. She pushed her chair back, rolled her neck, then the phone rang.

Jeff's voice answered her weary hello. "How you doing, Sis?"

"You don't really want to know." She put a hand on her side. Beneath her fingers, her scar throbbed.

"Sure, I do, that's why I'm calling. How about some Mexican food and beer? I'm heading over to La Paz. Come with me."

She considered his offer. Nothing sounded better than a cold Corona, but the reminders of Andres's calls glared at her from the corner of her desk. Two more had been added to the ones that had been waiting for her when she'd arrived. "Jeff, I'd love to, but you wouldn't believe the day I've had. I better head home and crash. I've got some thinking to do."

"Lots going on?"

"This and that."

"Have you found out any more about that Olvera fellow?"

"Not much."

"Doesn't that bother you? I mean, the guy shot you, after all."

"It's part of the job." Lena answered his questions with distraction. Thoughts of Andres made it impossible to concentrate on anything else. "Look, Jeff, I hate to cut this short…"

"No, it's okay. I understand completely. I'll call you next week and try again. How's that?"

"I'd love it."

"Great—we need to talk about Thanksgiving, too. You know, it's coming up."

Lena groaned. "Not again."

"Every year." She could hear the grin in his voice. "Dad called me yesterday to make sure I 'remembered' so you can expect your own summons shortly. Georgia Belle's getting wound up, too. I could hear her ranting and raving in the background when he phoned me."

Every year her father threw an enormous day-long party for Thanksgiving. It was basically a family affair but he also invited everyone from his law firm, including their children. His longtime housekeeper, Georgia Belle, grumbled about it for months before and months after, but she refused to let him cater it. It was her hams and turkeys, her pies and cakes, on the vast dining room table or no one's.

Lena hated the parties. Other than her brothers and their wives, she knew very few of the people who attended, and the ones she did know, she didn't care for. But her appearance was required.

As if reading her mind, Jeff spoke. "You will be there, right? Getting shot in the line of duty is no excuse, you know."

Lena had to laugh. "It almost might be worth it."

"You just don't know how to approach these things," Jeff responded. "I always try to find the most inappropriate date I can and that usually helps. Why don't you bring someone? Hell, bring Andres! That'd liven things up.''

Lena responded without thought as she recalled the tension between Andres and her father. ''Oh, no, Jeff. That's not a good idea, believe me.''

''What's wrong with inviting him? It might make the party bearable. Otherwise, the poor guy's gonna be all alone. No one should have to spend Thanksgiving in a rented condo.''

The image stopped her, especially after what Andres had told her about his family. Andres never said so, but surely he missed them even more on holidays.

''If you're saying no 'cause you think Dad will get pissed, that's probably true, but when has that prevented us from doing anything?''

Lena laughed again.

''If you're saying no because it might not be the right thing for you and Andres, then I guess I ought to butt out.'' In typical fashion, he then contradicted himself. ''*Are* you two getting closer?''

Lena closed her eyes. Closer? Yeah, you could use that word to describe their changing relationship...and a few others, too.

''I don't know,'' she lied. ''I'm just not sure it's a good idea to bring him to the house.''

''Well, it's your call,'' Jeff agreed. ''I'd certainly enjoy seeing him, but you know best.''

Lena hung up the phone slowly, her thoughts

confused and unsettled. A second later, right on cue, Andres walked into her office.

LENA LOOKED UP, surprise coming over her face. She wore her standard SWAT garb, a tight black T-shirt and slim black slacks, and she'd obviously had a rough day. He could see where she'd repeatedly run her hands through her hair and her lipstick was long gone. It didn't matter. A jolt of desire still went straight through him. It was the same kind of reaction he'd experienced when he'd first seen her on the plane, but this time it was even stronger.

He told himself he felt this way because of last night; his hands had caressed each curve and his lips had kissed all the secret places. His response wasn't simply physical though. Now it was emotional, as well.

But she hadn't called him back. His messages were spread across her desk like scattered leaves.

He paused on the threshold of the door. "Are you busy?"

"No, I'm finished. I was just about to go home."

They looked at each other with awkwardness. Andres knew what he wanted to say, knew what he wanted to do, but he had to tread lightly. He didn't want to scare her off.

"How was your day?" he asked. "I'm guessing very busy?"

She nodded, almost gratefully, he thought. "I was swamped." Lifting a hand toward her desk, she indicated the notes. "I'm sorry I couldn't call back."

"Don't worry about it. I figured you were tied up."

The superficial conversation dwindled into silence, and he walked over to her desk, stopping at the edge, close to where she stood. She let her eyes finally meet his.

"You have regrets?" he asked softly. "Over last night?"

His directness shocked her, he could tell. Shocked her so much she answered him truthfully. "No. I don't regret what happened."

"Good."

"But, Andres—"

He checked her words, putting a finger over her lips. "Stop there," he whispered. "Don't say anything else." Taking away his finger, he reached out and pulled her against him. She didn't resist. "I don't want to hear anything negative."

"How do you know it'd be negative?"

"Any sentence that starts with *but* is usually an argument I don't want to hear."

"But—"

"I know what you want to say, anyway." He ran his hands over her narrow back, feeling the taut muscles. "If you aren't going to say it was a mistake, then you want to tell me last night didn't

mean anything. You want to say what happened
between us was just sex and it won't happen again.
You want to take away what we shared, and I'm
not going to let you do that. When you opened
your door, you opened your heart, too. Let's don't
try to pretend you didn't.''

"Last night *was* just sex—"

He shook his head. "No. Sex is *never* just sex.
Not between us and you know it. It's never been
that way with you and that's one thing you can't
deny.''

The look on her face told him he'd hit a nerve.

"Maybe not." Her hands, resting on his shoulders, tightened. "But I'm not sure where I want
this to go, Andres. There are a lot of issues between us that we may never overcome.''

He hated what she said, but he understood. He'd
hurt her deeply, and any woman would be wary of
him. If there was a way he could clear the air between them, he would, but not at the cost she'd
have to pay. He refused to make Lena choose between him and her father.

She slipped out of his embrace and went to her
window. Silent for a moment, she finally turned
around. Her expression seemed uncertain, but
when she spoke, she spoke impulsively, almost as
if she were issuing herself a challenge.

"What are you doing for Thanksgiving?"

Her question took him by surprise. "Thanksgiving?"

"It's next week. Do you have plans?"

"Isabel is coming. She called and told me I'd bought her a ticket. She wants to see Destin."

Lena laughed. "Doesn't sound as if she's changed any."

"No, thank God, she hasn't. I haven't decided what I'd do with her, though. If you have any ideas…"

"Actually, I do. Remember the party, the one my father throws every year?" She shrugged apologetically. "It's kind of a madhouse, but it's required attendance for me. It's so huge you won't have to see him. Why don't you bring her to that?"

He couldn't help himself. He laughed out loud. "What an invitation! 'Please come to this party and you won't even have to see the host!'"

She grinned. "You'd be doing me a favor. And I think your aunt would like it."

Andres nodded. His *tia* did love to socialize, but underneath Lena's casual offer, there was more than a simple invitation. He knew it and so did she. Their eyes came together and the breezy exchange deepened into something more. He wasn't sure what, and she obviously wasn't, either, but they'd passed a certain point last night. Where they went from here depended on too many things to count. Maybe the invitation was a test.

If it was, Andres intended to pass.

"We'd be delighted to come to the party," he

KAY DAVID   155

answered. "I'll phone Isabel and tell her to pack
her best dress."

JEFF HAD CALLED it exactly right. As Lena headed
out to the parking lot following Andres's departure, her cell phone chirped. She glanced at the
display and saw Phillip's ID. For a moment she
considered not answering. She wanted to think
about Andres and the conversation they'd just
shared. He'd asked her out for dinner and she'd
turned him down. Accepting her answer without
argument, something he would never have done in
the past, he'd simply nodded.

But not before kissing her into oblivion. She'd
watched him leave afterward, feeling breathless
and more confused than ever.

She neared her car as the phone sounded again,
Punching one of the small, lighted buttons, she
said, "Hello, Dad."

"Lena, I'm calling about Thanksgiving. I want
you to plan on being at the house by nine."

No "hello," no "how are you," nothing in the
way of polite conversation. She juggled the phone
and the armful of reports she was taking home to
read, reaching out to unlock her car door.
"Thanksgiving?" she said innocently. "Is that
coming up already?"

"Don't be smart with me, Lena."

She threw the notebooks into her car where they
landed on the passenger seat then slid to the floor.

Rolling her eyes, she climbed inside. "Dad, I'm thirty-five years old. Don't talk to me as if I were twelve."

He ignored her answer as she knew he would. "All your brothers and their families will come at ten. I want you to come early so you can check on things. You have a good eye for detail. Just like your mother did. I want you there to make sure everything's been done right."

The unthinking demand, combined with the off-hand compliment and reference to Dorothea, was so typically Phillip that Lena shook her head. Carrot and stick. Love and hate. Push and pull.

She answered him as she usually did, by agreeing to what he wanted. "I'll be there, Dad." Starting her car, she kept it parked and gripped the phone tighter. "But I'm bringing a guest. Two actually."

"No problem. There'll be plenty for everyone. Who have you invited?"

Her mouth went dry and she reminded herself of what she'd just told him seconds before. She was thirty-five, for God's sake. A grown woman. If he didn't like who she was involved with, it was his problem, not hers.

"I'm bringing Andres," she said. "And his aunt. I'm sure you remember her, Isabel Gaspar. She's a lovely woman."

An icy silence built. She reached out and turned on the heater.

"What are you doing, Lena? Mounting some kind of petty rebellion just to upset me?"

"No." She answered serenely, and suddenly she realized her attitude wasn't just a ploy, she really did feel calm. If Phillip didn't approve, it wasn't important. What mattered most was what was happening between her and Andres. *That* was what she had to work out. "Jeff suggested it and after thinking about it, I asked Andres. He accepted the invitation."

"Are you telling me you're seeing this bastard again, Lena?"

"I'm telling you I've invited him to the house for Thanksgiving."

"That's not what I asked you."

"No, but that's the answer you're getting. If you don't like it, I'll uninvite him. It is *your* party. But I'd feel an obligation to have them to my place instead."

"And not come to the house."

"That's right."

He said nothing and in the quiet Lena repeated to herself the same question he'd just asked. What in the *hell* was she doing? She wasn't even sure she wanted Andres at the party, much less back in her life again, but here she was standing up for him. One thing made about as much sense as the other.

Her father spoke again. "This was Jeff's idea?"

"He mentioned it, yes. But I'm the one who asked Andres."

She switched off the heater. All at once, it seemed too warm.

"All right." Phillip seemed suddenly weary. "You can bring the son of a bitch, but I don't like it, Lena. I don't like it one damn bit. You're asking for more trouble and a broken heart to boot. When he hurts you again—and he will—you remember that I warned you."

REACHING FOR HIS fourth cup of coffee, Andres tried to focus on the reports spread out in front of him. He was sitting at the dining table of his condo, the sound of the ocean a distant murmur. He'd left Lena's office hours ago, but in his mind, he was back in her bed, his arms wrapped around her slender body, his lips buried against her neck.

Her invitation to her father's party had been completely unexpected, and Andres still wasn't too sure what it meant. From the way she'd given it, he decided she wasn't too sure, either. It seemed as if she were trying to judge where they were and what was happening between them by issuing the offer.

One thing was for sure. He'd made an important, if inadvertent, point when he'd told her what had happened between them wasn't just sex. Those gray eyes had widened and she'd blinked—in that funny way she could—telling him he'd expressed not only how he felt, but how she felt, too. She could try to deny it all she wanted; he knew the truth, and in her heart, she did, too. Their connection was as strong now as it'd ever been, maybe even stronger. No matter what secrets he kept from her, the bond would always be there.

He rocked back in his chair then stood and crossed the room to the balcony doors. Pushing open the heavy glass, he stepped out onto the patio. Tiled and bordered by a sturdy metal railing, it ran the length of the condo. He walked to the edge and stared out into the darkness, the sound of the waves louder now that he was outside.

Maybe it was time to tell her the truth.

And maybe not.

After a moment, he accepted reality; his speculation was pointless. With a disgusted curse, he turned and went back inside, slamming the door behind him. He might as well get back to work and see if he could make any progress there.

He returned to the scattered reports. It took a while, but he finally managed to focus his thoughts, his fingers shifting through the papers until he found the ones he wanted. The notes from Carmen.

Using the cops' listings, she'd fed the license plate numbers and car models of the vehicles seen at the Silver Shores Motel into the database in Miami.

Three had been registered in Dade County. One

was a rental, registered to a retired tailor from New York who'd come to Destin to fish. The second vehicle was a van owned by a man and his wife who were visiting relatives nearby. The final vehicle, the abandoned car Andres had told Lena about in the hospital, had been "borrowed" by a teenaged couple who'd run off to get married. Ultimately, none of the cars under surveillance had any connection to the Red Tide.

But Carmen was sharp. One local vehicle had been seen in the vicinity several times, she noted. Three times to be exact. The first time had been just after the surveillance had begun, the second time a few days later, early one morning. In the third and final instance, the car hadn't stopped but had cruised through quickly. Since it hadn't parked, the cops hadn't noted its presence but Carmen had. She'd studied the photo sheets. The vehicle had been captured passing through the parking lot just as one of the officers had snapped the row of parked cars.

She'd traced the number and make of the late-model silver Lincoln. It was registered to a business in Niceville, a small town just north of Destin off Highway 285.

AAA Bail Bonds.

The name meant nothing to Andres, and probably meant nothing, period. For all he knew the car belonged to a frustrated bounty hunter meeting up with a local hooker. Or maybe it was an unfaithful husband and his girlfriend coming together at the Silver Shores.

He tossed the report to one side and made a mental note. He'd call Carmen in the morning and tell her to track down the owners of AAA and see who they were. Most likely a dead end, but worth a try. The Red Tide frequently worked through legitimate businesses.

He went to bed an hour later. Lena was beside him, but only in his dreams.

CHAPTER TEN

SHE DIDN'T dress up often.

Standing in front of her closet a week later, Lena glared at the choices as if it were their fault nothing seemed adequate for her father's Thanksgiving party.

She ran her hand through the hangers one more time. She was taking so much time, she knew she'd be late, but she didn't really care. Selecting the right thing to wear meant more to her than Phillip's certain irritation.

The red jacket and skirt? Too businesslike. She only wore it to the various conferences she attended as a representative of the team. The black silk pantsuit? Too severe. It was her marry-and-bury suit. She pulled it out for weddings and funerals.

From the back row, something caught her eye and she pushed aside her jeans to get to it.

It was her navy dress. The sparkly one. The last time she'd worn it was the night before the wedding.

Her fingers closed around the hanger and she

removed the gown. Holding it up to her body, she turned slowly and looked in the mirror behind her. The heat in Andres's eyes when she'd worn it that evening was something she'd always remember. Oh, she'd pushed it aside, of course, like she'd pushed away all the good memories of their times together, but it was there all the same. Waiting, watching, daring her to resurrect it.

Impulsively, she threw off her bathrobe and slipped the dress over her head. It was a little loose, because she'd lost some weight, but the sheath still fit.

Turning slowly, she studied herself in the mirror and ran her hands over her sides, smoothing the seams. The garment was more than just a dress— it held all the promise of what had been before them. Their life together. Their marriage. The unborn children that were sure to come.

Lena cursed softly. Andres had had to go to Washington for a few days and they hadn't spoken since he'd returned. But she didn't need to talk to him to understand that she was torturing herself. The past always replayed itself, one way or the other. If she let Andres in her life once more, it wouldn't be the good times that came with him— it'd be the bad. He'd make her love him again and then he'd leave her. Her speculations ran together, connected by a string of confusion. She didn't trust him and he didn't trust her and nothing had

changed so why would it work now when it didn't
back then?

She was crazy if she thought the relationship
would be different now. Great sex didn't mean a
damned thing. It was great sex and nothing else.

Closing her heart and shutting off her mind, she
yanked the dress over her head and marched across
the bedroom to the phone. She picked up the receiver, dialed his number and practiced what she'd
say.

*I'm sorry, Andres, but I think it'd be best for
you not to come.... I'm sorry, Andres, but the situation has changed.... I'm sorry, Andres...but
please don't come today. I don't want you there....*

The phone rang emptily—he'd obviously gone
to the airport to pick up his aunt. They'd go
straight from there to Phillip's. Cursing once again,
Lena hung up, her real message sounding only inside her head.

*I'm sorry, Andres, but I think I'm falling in love
with you again...I just can't let that happen.*

RAMROD STRAIGHT and every detail in place, Isabel Gaspar was the first person off the plane. She
wore her standard garb; a severe black dress and
three-inch heels. Her hair was pulled back and
twisted into a single bun, pinned at the nape of her
neck. The model of a fashionable older woman, her
appearance was almost Spartan until a huge smile
warmed her expression as she spotted Andres. He

realized at once how much he'd missed her the past few weeks. In Miami, they met at least once a month. He'd take her out to one of the nice Cuban restaurants she loved or shopping in one of the glittering malls. She'd raised Andres after his mother had died and it'd been her encouragement that had propelled him to leave Cuba. They were very close.

They embraced tightly, then she looked at him critically, her eyes going over his face. "You look tired," she announced, her Spanish fluid. "You're working too hard, I assume?"

He laughed and draped his arm around her shoulder. "I'm working like I always do."

She nodded. "Too hard."

In the luggage area, he grabbed her case then led her out the door to the parking lot. She tugged her sweater closer. "It's colder here than Miami."

"Destin is much farther north. And on the Gulf of Mexico. But the water is spectacular. You'll love it. Emerald green and smooth."

They continued the casual conversation until they were in the black Suburban and heading toward Phillip's house. Then Andres felt her black eyes drilling his profile.

"So you're seeing Lena again, eh? I'm surprised she let you near her. You hurt her deeply, Andres."

Isabel knew the truth. He'd told her everything.

"I know, I know." He glanced toward her. "I didn't have a choice, *Tia*."

She pursed her lips in disapproval. "Don't give me that. Everyone has choices."

He didn't try to argue with her; she'd win because she always won—and because she was right.

"Would you like to stop by my place and freshen up or go straight to the party?"

"Don't ignore me," she said sharply. "I'm not going to pretend your past with Lena does not exist. I'm too old for such nonsense."

He reached across the car seat and patted her hand. "No one could ignore you, *Tia*, believe me. I don't have an answer, that's all."

"Then perhaps it's time you find one. You're growing old, and so am I. Before I die, I want to sit in the sunshine with some little ones on my lap."

LENA PULLED INTO Phillip's driveway and angled her truck into the first empty spot she found, a narrow patch of pavement close to the sidewalk. The circular turnaround was already full of her brothers' Mercedes-Benzes and BMWs. Her Ford looked as out of place as Jeff's Toyota, which was in the street, next to the curb. He hadn't even tried to park near the house. As she slammed her car door and locked it, she couldn't help but shake her head. What a metaphor for how they all related…

She started up the sidewalk and smoothed her dress, a dark-green silk that she'd dragged from the back of the closet in desperation. Her thoughts turned again to Andres. Why on earth had she invited him here today? She thought briefly of trying to call him one more time. It would be past rude at this point, though. He was due any minute.

By the time she reached the front porch, she could hear the crowd inside. With a grimace of distaste, she opened the door.

Phillip materialized just as Lena slipped off her jacket and hung it in the hall closet. For a while after Dorothea's death, her fur had dangled, abandoned in the back. Lena would sneak into the darkness and press her face against its satin folds, seeking some comfort from it. Phillip had found her there one day and the next time she'd looked for the coat, the garment was gone.

He brushed her cheek with his, then eyed her outfit in a way that told her she'd made a bad choice. "You're late," he said brusquely. "I wanted you here early—"

"I know what you wanted, Dad." Glancing in the mirror, Lena ran a hand through her hair and tried to tame it before giving up. "I'm sorry. I ran out of time."

He waved away her excuse, as quick to forgive as he was to criticize. "It doesn't matter," he said. "Lucy came and checked things out for me."

Lena held back a groan. Lucy was Bering's wife. Quiet, shy and totally cowed by her husband, she did exactly what he told her to, and since Bering's biggest dream was to move into Phillip's house, he made Lucy "help" Phillip every time he had the opportunity. Lena wasn't surprised at anything Bering did these days. He was definitely getting pushier, though. She didn't like his aggressiveness, but she kept her opinion to herself.

"How nice," Lena said neutrally, "that Lucy could do that for you."

Ignoring her reply, Phillip took Lena's arm and steered her toward a corner of the entry, deftly dodging two of her nephews who ran by, screaming at each other at the top of their lungs. They were Patty and Richard's, Lena noted, and totally out of control, as always. Patty was a stay-at-home mom who'd given up a lucrative law practice of her own to raise their children. She should have stuck with her torts.

"Is Casimiro still coming?" Phillip's hand tightened on Lena's arm.

"As far as I know, yes, he is."

"Well, I want you to know I don't approve."

Lena sighed. "I'm aware of how you feel."

"You have no idea how I feel, Lena." He clutched the baluster of the stair beside them, his knuckles going white. "None whatsoever—"

The doorbell sounded behind them, and Stephanie, Steven's wife, bustled into the entry, called by the tones. Competent and organized, she ran her home like the military one she'd come from herself. She nodded a quick hello to Lena. "Shall I get that, Papa?"

"Yes, please." He put his hand back on Lena's arm and dropped his voice. "All I'm trying to do is protect you, Lena. That's all. I love you and I don't want you hurt. There are things you don't understand about this situation. Things I should have told you."

Behind them, Lena heard the front door open. "I *do* understand, Dad, more than you realize. But I'm a grown woman now and I have to make my own decisions. That's the bottom line and—" She broke off suddenly, the noise of the arriving guests finally registering. Phillip's expression snapped closed and without a word, he turned and left. Lena whirled and met Andres's eyes.

Her pulse began to thunder before she could control herself. He wore a black double-breasted suit with a white shirt and a gleaming red silk tie. All she could think about was the time they'd spent in her bed.

He crossed the marble floor and kissed both her cheeks, his lips warm as they brushed her skin, his hands reassuring as they took hers. He said nothing, but led her back to the front door where his aunt stood.

"Mrs. Gaspar! How wonderful to see you again." Lena smiled at the older woman and accepted her kisses, too. "Did you have a good flight?"

"It was very good, thank you." Her voice, heavily accented, was quiet and refined as she looked around the entry. "What a lovely home. It was nice of you to include us today."

"I'm glad you could come."

Lena looked cool and collected and incredibly beautiful, the deep green of her dress the perfect complement to her hair and eyes. He wanted to take her into his arms and kiss her until neither of them knew where they were. But he couldn't.

Lena stepped closer and took Isabel's arm. With their heads bent together, the two women walked toward the living room. Andres watched them go and wondered what he'd done by coming here. He didn't have too long to think about it as Jeff entered the hallway and greeted him.

"So you made it!" Jeff shook Andres's hand. "You're a brave man."

"Brave or stupid? I'm not too sure which, my friend."

Jeff laughed. "Sometimes that's one and the same, you know. At least with my sister, it is. And I have the scars to prove it."

He rolled up the right sleeve of his sweater. A small white line bisected his forearm. "That's where she caught me with the business end of a sword we weren't supposed to touch." He pushed down his sleeve and pointed to his chin. "And this is where she got me with a tennis racket when I was fifteen. It's a good thing I went off to school when I turned eighteen. I might not have survived much longer."

Andres chuckled. "Phillip did nothing to protect you, eh?"

"Protect me?" Lena's brother made a scoffing sound. "Lena could have killed me and Dad would never have noticed. The only time he paid any attention to the rest of us was when he took us hunting, and I had to get a twenty point buck with one shot before he even acknowledged me." He shook his head. "Lena was always his favorite."

Jeff was clearly joking, but just beneath the surface, Andres heard a touch of sibling rivalry. It was no secret, even though their relationship was a perplexing labyrinth of love and hate, Phillip had always favored Lena over the boys. And the other brothers over Jeff. He *was* at the bottom of the hierarchy no matter how it was viewed.

As if realizing he was getting too close to the truth, Jeffrey abruptly dropped the subject and steered Andres into the crowd, introducing him to everyone. The crush of lawyers from Phillip's office and their families relieved Andres from saying little more than hello to Lena's other brothers, although Bering had enough time to send him a particularly nasty look. Jeff stayed by his side as if he understood the potential awkwardness of the situation. But he couldn't stop the inevitable. Phillip met them near the back of the room, close to the French doors that led to the garden.

"Go check on the table, Jeffrey." Phillip didn't

look at his son as he spoke. He only stared at Andres. "I want to talk to Mr. Casimiro."

Andres felt Jeff hesitate, but there was little he could do other than comply. He eased back into the crowd and left them alone.

"Let's step outside," Phillip said. "I don't want to be overheard."

Andres followed the old man into the weak fall sun. They crossed a slate-covered patio and stopped just before the steps that led down to the pool. Crystal clear and shimmering, the turquoise water looked cold and uninviting. Andres folded his arms, raised his eyebrows, and waited for Phillip to speak. He was angry and about to erupt.

The explosion came quickly.

"I want to know just what in the hell you think you're doing." Phillip's blue eyes held fire.

"Attending a dinner party?" Andres ventured.

"That's not what I mean and you know it. Don't give me that innocent act, dammit."

Truly mystified, Andres shook his head. "You must be losing it, Phillip. I have no idea what you're talking about."

"Save your bullshit, I'm not buying it." He reached inside his coat pocket and pulled out a pink phone slip. "I have proof and if you don't cease and desist, I'm filing on you, make no doubt about it."

Andres reached out and took the note from the lawyer's fingers. The scribbled notation told him little other than the fact that Carmen had called Phillip's office last week. Puzzled, Andres shook his head. "I don't know what this is about, Phillip."

"You're having this woman harass me for no good purpose."

"Harass you?"

"That's right. She called my offices last week and insisted on talking to me. When my secretary refused, she somehow managed to obtain my private number and called me directly." His face flushed. "I know you're behind this, dammit, so don't act so naive."

Andres frowned. "What did Carmen want with you?"

"You're telling me you don't know about this?"

"That's exactly what I'm telling you."

For the first time, Lena's father looked hesitant. "She wanted information about some of my businesses," he answered. "I hold primary interest in a number of concerns besides the law firm. Investments I've made through the years. I haven't been active in some of them for quite some time and in others, never." He narrowed his eyes, his irritation returning. "I told her to go to hell and that's the same message I have for you."

"I have no idea what she was doing, Phillip."

"You expect me to believe that?"

"It's the truth." Andres shrugged. "Believe what you will."

Phillip turned and looked out over the pool. He thought quietly for a moment, then he glanced at Andres again. "We go back a long way."

Andres waited.

"And you're sleeping with my daughter."

The words ignited Andres's own anger. "That's personal and none of your business! You have no right—"

"I may not have the right, but it's the truth." A ray of sunshine hit his silver hair and highlighted the wrinkles pulling down his face. "Don't try to tell me you aren't because I know. I can tell just by looking at her. And I know where it's probably going to lead, too. I'll fight it every step of the way, though—make no mistake about it."

"You're jumping to conclusions, *viejo.*"

"Say what you must," Phillip answered, "but I disagree. That's why I need to know the truth once and for all. If you're investigating me—*again*— let's put the cards on the table and get the evidence out in the open."

He knew.

A wave of shock rippled over Andres at the revelation. Phillip *knew* Andres had investigated him for Mateo's murder.

"I want to know, Casimiro. I want the truth." He focused on Andres's face with all the intensity of a time-tested interrogator. "You tell me right here and now why you have so many questions about AAA Bail Bonds."

ISABEL SAT QUIETLY on the sofa and nodded as
Lena explained to her who the various guests were.
When Lena finished, Andres's aunt spoke softly.
"You have a large family. How nice for you."

Lena immediately remembered Andres's words
about his mother. "It can be nice," she said with
a smile. "But you know how brothers and sisters
get along. I'm closest to Jeff, but sometimes the
others get to me. Did you have that problem?"

She smiled gently. "Of course. Yolanda, Andres's mother, and I had our disagreements. It was
just the two of us, though. We had no brothers or
other sisters. We would have loved it if there had
been more, but now I guess it worked out as it
should. I could never have left the island if I'd had
relatives still there."

Lena nodded. "Was it difficult for you to
leave?"

"Not in terms of going, no. I'd had my fill of
what they were doing—still do—to the people.
And of course I wanted to be near Andres since
he's the only one I have left." Her dark eyes
turned soft. "I do miss the island itself, though.
The warm winds, the blue sky, the green water…"

"Andres loved it."

"Oh, yes, he did. When he was a little boy he
said he would never leave. That he would grow up
and be a fisherman just like his *papá*. Every day
he would go out on the boat with Angelo. It made

Yolanda nervous, but she said nothing." Her voice sharpened. "My sister was a good Spanish wife."

Lena looked at Isabel curiously. "What do you mean?"

"She never said anything to Angelo that would make him unhappy. She existed only because of him." The older woman pulled a lace-edged handkerchief from the inside of her sleeve. Folding it twice, she twined it around her fingers. "It cost her her life."

"Her life?"

"She dared to complain when Angelo persisted with his activities with the underground. He quickly told her it was man's work and to stay out of it so she did. Then he was arrested. He rotted in prison for ten years while she pined away. She needed him to live. When he died, she followed shortly."

Isabel looked across the room, but Lena knew she wasn't really seeing the crowd. "She should have been a stronger woman," she said softly. "She should have needed him less and depended on herself more. She had a child she should have lived for. Instead, she died and I raised him." Blinking, Isabel seemed to come out of her past. She turned to Lena, reached out and patted her on the knee. "She should have been like you, *chica*. An independent woman who needs no one but herself."

Lena protested without thinking. "I'm not that

self-assured, Isabel, believe me. I may have a tough job, but I also have more than my share of self-doubt."

"Andres doesn't think so. He sees you as totally independent."

"He always has."

"Why do you think so?"

"I don't know," Lena replied. "He sees the outer me and assumes it's the inner me, as well. Deep down, I'm as shaky as the next guy, but I can't let that out."

"Because of your job?"

"That's part of it." It was Lena's turn to look across the room. Her father was holding court, telling one of his stories to a crowd of attorneys. She nodded toward him. "The rest of it goes back to my childhood, I suppose. After my mom died things changed. I wasn't the youngest, but I was the only girl, and if I showed any kind of weakness or neediness, it was pounced on by my father *and* my brothers. I *had* to be independent to survive. It became my habit, I guess. My protective armor. I think I simply picked a job that matched my attitude."

"So you always must be the strong one, yes? Never let them see you cry?"

As Isabel spoke, Lena thought back to the conversation in her office the day Brandon had been hurt. She'd told Andres how she felt, confessed to her self-doubt. She'd allowed him to see her true emotions.

And he hadn't mocked her; he'd understood completely. He'd understood, then he'd comforted her, in just the right way, and finally he'd kissed her. She'd let down her guard and needed him, and he'd come through for her in the best possible manner.

It was a realization that would stay with her for the rest of the day.

CHAPTER ELEVEN

SITTING AT THE dinner table an hour later, Andres glanced down the expanse of mahogany in Phillip's direction. Clearly feeling the heat of the stare, the attorney turned his head sharply and glared back.

Although he hadn't revealed it, Andres had been shocked by Phillip's question on the balcony, the pieces of the puzzle clicking into place with alarming alacrity. "I can't answer questions about current investigations," he'd replied automatically.

"Then you *are* investigating me?"

"I didn't say that. Don't twist my words."

"I'll twist any damn thing I want to," the old man had said angrily. "And when this is finished, it'll be your neck."

Andres reached for his wineglass and felt a stare of his own. He didn't have to look up to know it came from Lena. She'd seen him reenter the living room a few minutes after Phillip, and going to his side, she'd wanted to know what they'd been talking about.

"The usual," he'd said laconically. She hadn't

accepted his answer, and even now he could sense her curiosity from across the table.

It hardly mattered. Connecting that Lincoln Town Car to AAA Bail Bonds meant connecting Phillip McKinney to the Silver Shores Motel. And the Silver Shores Motel meant one thing and one thing only to Andres. The Red Tide.

He couldn't believe Carmen hadn't told him what she was doing. She knew nothing, of course, about his prior investigation of McKinney but she should have recognized the importance of this information. He'd tried to call her early this morning, but she hadn't answered. Why hadn't she said anything about this to him last week?

The rich wine suddenly felt heavy on his tongue. Carmen still had family in Havana, and many times they'd discussed the situation—the unstable atmosphere, the uncertainty of life on the island. She'd voiced opinions about the political upheaval there, but he hadn't listened that closely. Now he wished he had. Could she somehow be involved with the Red Tide? God, if she was, it meant she had conned Isabel and Andres both. What was she doing?

What was Phillip doing?

Andres looked down the table again. Ever since Mateo had died, he'd wanted to connect Phillip McKinney to his best friend's murder. Now he had a concrete link between McKinney and a known member of the organization—Esteban Olvera. Not

just any member, either, but the one who'd been
sent to kill Andres. He should be overjoyed but he
wasn't. He simply had more questions than ever
before, the most important of which he hardly
dared to consider.

Wrapping his fingers around his goblet, Andres
turned his head again to meet Lena's puzzled eyes.
There was something special in her gaze, and all
at once, he accepted the fact that Phillip *was* right
about one thing. Andres did love Lena.

He loved her as much as her father hated him.

SOMETHING WAS bothering Andres.

From above the flickering candles, Lena stared
at him, pretending all the time that she was listening to the woman at her left. Intense and way too
focused, she was one of Phillip's young attorneys,
and she was doing her best to ingratiate herself to
Lena. She had no idea Lena was ignoring her.

He'd been fine before he'd gone outside with
Phillip. Lena peeked toward her father. He was
deep in conversation with one of his partners but
as she watched, he turned in her direction. It wasn't
her he was trying to see, though; it was Andres,
she realized a moment later. Andres raised his
eyes, and an arc of tension stretched between the
two men. Lena felt caught between them in more
ways than one.

She decided right then and there she was going
to get to the bottom of their problem, one way or

the other. She'd insist one of them tell her the truth and if he didn't, then she'd go to the other. Enough was enough.

A second later, Lena's pager, tucked into the pocket of her dress, began to vibrate. Excusing herself, she reached down and pulled it out. The code number it displayed sent her abruptly to her feet. Her father looked at her with an inquiring glance.

"I have to go," she announced. "I'm sorry, but it's an emergency." She dropped her napkin on her chair and headed out to the hallway. Andres met her in the center of the entry as she jerked her coat from the closet.

"Let me drive you," he said, reaching for his own jacket.

She automatically started to decline then she stopped. She'd have to change clothes. If he drove her, she could switch in the car and be there even faster. "That would help," she said. "But what about Isabel—"

"I asked Jeff to drop her by the hotel. He said it would be no problem. And someone from the office can get the SUV and drop it at my condo."

She nodded. "All right, then, let's go."

Their footsteps echoed on the marble as they strode out the door. Fifteen minutes later, they were speeding down Highway 98 in Lena's truck. From the back, Lena grabbed the spare uniform she always kept in a bag, then began to peel off her panty hose.

Andres glanced across the seat, his black eyes gleaming. "This could be interesting."

"Keep driving." Her voice was muffled by her dress as she yanked it over her head and quickly replaced it with a black sweatshirt. "I want us to get there in one piece. You, especially. I have some questions and I want some answers."

"I've had enough questions from McKinneys today, *por favor*..."

She retrieved her boots from the rear floorboard and a pair of socks. "That's exactly what I want to ask you about. What were you and my father discussing outside, Andres? The tension between you two is unbelievable."

"He wanted some information about a case. Something I'm working on. I couldn't tell him, of course, and that made him mad."

"A case? The only thing you're working on is the Red Tide thing, right? What would he want with—"

"Our office has more than one investigation going on, Lena."

She stuck a clip in her mouth then used both hands to pull back her hair. Holding the strands to one side, she reclaimed the clip and secured it at the back of her head. "Tell me more," she demanded.

"Tell me where to take you. I'll fill you in later."

"Fill me in now." She took out her beeper and read off the address.

He ignored her demand, his reaction immediate. "Are you kidding? About that address?"

"No." Puzzled by his voice, she shook her head and looked at the flashing window again. "That's the number and the street. 1990 Gulf Shore Drive, Number 403. It's a condo complex. Someone saw a guy going into one of the units then they heard shots. The P.D. came but the intruder apparently started shooting back and they can't get any closer." She stopped. "What do you know about the building?"

"That's Emerald Towers South." He glanced across the seat, his eyes going dark. "That's where Carmen lives. In Number 403."

LENA JUMPED OUT before Andres had the vehicle fully stopped. "I'll call you after I know what's going on—"

"No way." Andres put the truck in park, then climbed out as well. He slammed and locked the door, staring at her from over the hood. "I'm coming."

"Andres! You can't come. This is a SWAT operation—"

"And I'm Justice with an employee who might be involved. I'm coming, Lena."

It was futile for her to argue. With a curse, she

turned sharply and headed toward the Winnebago down the street. He followed right behind her.

As they entered the War Wagon, Bradley glanced up. He nodded as Lena explained Andres's connection to Carmen. Sarah Greenberg stood in the back and listened as well.

"Give me all her personal information," Sarah demanded. "I need to know everything I can about her."

Andres and the young cop began to talk as Lena grabbed the headset Bradley held out to her. "Tell me how this started," she said.

"As a cluster-screw, basically," Bradley answered, shaking his head. "Resident calls the switchboard an hour ago and says she thinks her neighbor's been shot. She saw the woman's boyfriend go into the condo, then she heard something that sounded like gunfire a few minutes later. The P.D. happens to have a unit down the street. They're here in seconds, they come up the elevator, knock on the door, and shots are fired— through the door—no warning whatsoever. Instead of going in, they take cover and now we're stuck. It's a miracle no one was hit."

Lena felt her gut tighten. Reaching for the binoculars, she focused on the fourth floor of the highrise building in front of them. This was her worst nightmare. For years she'd worried about something happening in one of the densely packed condominium towers that dotted the beach. The majority of them had a single elevator with stairwells at both ends. If he had enough ammo, a hostage taker could hold off an army for days. The people at risk would be the closest civilians.

Bradley seemed to read her mind. "The neighbor who called is a widow who lives by herself on the right side of 403. On the left are renters. Two families from Texas—two couples, five kids. There are five other residents on that floor. We got out the two nearest the stairwells but we're afraid to move the rest."

"Keep them where they are for now." She dropped the glasses and spoke into her headset. "Check in, please."

The men answered in rotation. Two in each stairwell. One beside the elevator. Diego on standby in the lobby. The telephone wasn't working inside the unit. He'd been up once and tried the bullhorn but no one had answered.

Behind them, Sarah spoke up, a phone in her hand. "The unit above 403 is empty," she said excitedly. "I just talked to the management firm. We can get guys in there."

"Do it."

Bradley spit out instructions into his microphone. Listening to the conversation, Lena heard the men respond. They were already prepared and had the mirrors with them. In seconds, they'd be above the unit and with any luck, able to see inside.

The radio continued to crackle softly as she glanced to where Andres stood in the back of the bus. Underneath his calm demeanor, she could tell he was worried. For a single second, she felt a flash of jealousy; Carmen was gorgeous, they worked together closely. From the first time she'd seen the woman on the plane Lena had known how she felt about Andres. Did he know, too? How did he feel about her? The widow had mentioned a boy-friend....

"She has two kids." Andres answered Lena's unspoken questions. "She's divorced." Pausing for a second, he seemed to think about something, then he spoke again. "She doesn't have a boy-friend."

"Well, she's obviously seeing someone," Lena said. "The neighbor must have seen the guy coming and going if she's calling him a boyfriend."

"I don't know about that. But I do know she was not dating anyone here." He paused, then spoke again, almost haltingly. "She was checking on some things for me about the Red Tide case. Following a lead I didn't know anything about. I just found out she was doing this tonight."

An uneasy feeling came over Lena. "What kind of lead?"

"A local tie-in," he said tensely.

Before Lena could query him further, a voice came through her headset, speaking quietly. Her attention immediately left Andres and she focused on the words, her fingers pressing her earpiece closer.

"We're in." It was Scott. "Linc is going to the balcony to drop the mirrors."

"Easy, Linc," Bradley spoke urgently. "You can hear those balcony doors open from below."

"Ten-four."

Unlike Brandon, Linc was a seasoned veteran; he knew what he was doing. Lena turned back to Andres, her voice tense. "Surely there's something else you can tell us, Andres. Anything—"

"I've got him." Linc's voice broke into Lena's headset.

Something in his tone alerted her, and all at once Lena forgot about Andres.

"I can see through a crack in the drapes. They're parted just a bit. He's by the front door, looking out the peephole."

"How many?"

"Just one."

"What about the woman?" Lena felt Andres's eyes on her face as she spoke into her mike. "Can you see her?"

The answer was professional and curt. "She's on the couch. She's dead."

Lena dropped her gaze. "Keep your mirrors steady and hang tight."

She pulled back her mouthpiece and looked up. Andres read her expression, then pivoted and cursed. Bradley and Sarah stood by quietly. Lena tilted her head toward the front of the bus. They moved past her, and she went to the rear of the narrow aisle, where Andres waited, his head bowed.

Feeling guilty for her earlier jealous thoughts, Lena put her hand on his shoulder. "I'm sorry." Andres shook his head and said nothing. "Had she been with you a long time?"

It took him a second to answer. "About a year, more or less. She was a friend of Isabel's and that's why I hired her. Her kids—" He stopped and cleared his throat. "Her kids are staying with her father while she's working here. I'll call him when this is over. I have the number."

"Do you want me to do it?"

"I will. Their father works overseas, and Carmen's dad will have to track him down." He raised his head and stared out the window. "This is all my fault."

She spoke automatically. "This isn't your fault, Andres. Don't say that."

He turned around, his expression tortured. "Yes, it is. Trust me, Lena. If I hadn't—"

He stopped himself abruptly and Lena felt a knife twist inside her. What kind of feelings had he had for Carmen? Was she in Destin to work for him or did their relationship go deeper?

"L1, we got trouble!"

Lena yanked her mike toward her mouth, but Linc was speaking again before she could say anything. "The patio doors just opened downstairs. He's standing by the railing and—goddammit, he's climbing up. Shit! No, man, wait... No—"

The cop's voice broke off abruptly, and in the background, Lena heard a scream. Then silence.

"L1?"

"I'm here, Lincoln." Lena gripped the mouthpiece with her fingers as Andres moved closer to her. "What happened?"

"He just jumped! I guess he was trying to make it to the balcony below but he missed." She heard the wind whistling into the cop's mike as he obviously leaned out to look over. It made for an eerie sound. He finally spoke again, his voice weary. "Call for the wagon. He's dead."

IT WAS AFTER midnight by the time they wrapped up the scene. From an out-of-the-way spot nearby, Andres watched Lena direct the various men and handle the debriefing. He'd already called Carmen's family. Sarah had dealt with the news media. They'd descended on the condos immediately, their microphones thrust before them, the anchors made up and ready. Even now, looking through the crowd, he could spot the print guys still hanging around, hoping for another tidbit. The television crews had left a little after ten. They'd done their live remotes for the late news then disappeared. The dead man had no identification on him and without that, the reporters no longer appeared to care.

What did it all mean? Andres wondered emptily. If Carmen had been involved with the Red Tide, where did that leave them now?

If she hadn't been connected to them, the questions were even more confusing.

Lena navigated the crowded parking lot, lifted the yellow crime scene ribbon at the edge, and came to Andres's side. She threaded her hand through her hair, her face wearing a look of total exhaustion.

"Come home with me," he said suddenly. "My place is one block over. It'd take half an hour to go out to your house."

She shocked him by agreeing.

They pulled into his complex five minutes later. He thought briefly of telling her his suspicions about Carmen, then he swallowed his words. He had to be sure before he threw out an accusation that serious. Lena stayed silent during the elevator ride up to his floor and remained that way until they entered his unit.

Stepping inside, she looked around. "Very nice."

"Carmen picked it out." He regretted the comment the minute it was out of his mouth. It seemed to thrust them both right back into the horror.

Lena simply nodded and headed to the back, the obvious direction of his bedroom and bath. He heard the sound of the shower running, and fifteen minutes later she came out, wrapped in his bathrobe. She walked directly to him and stood so close he could smell the shampoo she'd used, so close he could see the drops of water still hanging on her eyelashes. She looked younger and even more vulnerable. She spoke huskily, as if the words hurt.

"Were you sleeping with her?"

It took a moment for him to understand, and another to form his reply.

"What makes you think I was sleeping with Carmen?"

"I'm not sure that *is* what I think," Lena replied. "But something's not right here. What is it?"

He put his hands on either side of her face. Her skin was moist and warm. "I wasn't sleeping with her…."

She nodded, her expression easing minutely.

"But I had."

She stiffened and started to pull away, but he refused to let her go. His hands on her shoulders, he held her in place. "I'm not going to lie to you, Lena. You asked me so you're getting the truth."

Her eyes filled with pain. "Right. And next you'll tell me it was a mistake, and it only happened once."

"It was, and it did." He tightened his grip. "It should never have happened."

"You're a grown man. You're not married. It's all right."

"No, it's not." He rubbed his thumbs over her arms, the silky robe too thin to hold her heat. "I shouldn't have slept with her…because I still loved you." He paused. "I love you now. I always have. And I always will."

Lena felt her heart stutter to a stop.

Dropping his hands, he stepped back as he spoke, his expression angry. "I wanted you but you weren't there and she was. That doesn't make it right—in fact, it makes it worse—but that's the truth. When I realized it, I told her it wouldn't happen again, and it didn't."

"You love me?" Lena repeated the words stupidly.

"Of course I love you!" He pushed his hands through his hair. "My God, Lena, you couldn't tell that the other night?"

"I thought it was just…"

"Just sex? I told you already that wasn't the case. Do you really think so little of me?"

"I didn't know!"

Abruptly, he drew her to him. She could feel his fury as she raised her hands and put them on his chest.

"How many times do I have to say it? It's never been just sex between us, Lena, and you know it. Every time I touch you, every time you touch me, something happens between us, something that goes way beyond the physical. It's what makes our relationship work, it's what holds us together, even when we've been apart. Surely you know that by now.''

His words and his intensity shook her. "But I thought—"

"You don't have to think about it, dammit. You do that too much. You *shouldn't* think about it." He flattened his hands on her back, his accent intensifying. "Just love me back. That's all you have to do."

She parted her lips to speak, to say something although she didn't know what, but he lowered his mouth to hers and began to kiss her. It was a needy kiss, a demanding kiss, a kiss that told her more than any words he could have said.

And God help her, she kissed him back.

He dropped his hands to her buttocks and pulled her closer, almost lifting her off the ground. She responded by wrapping her arms around his neck, the feel of his hair soft beneath her curling fingers. Moaning into his open mouth, Lena knew she was lost once more. Set into motion, the passion between them took on a life of its own. Nothing could have stopped it. She didn't care if he'd slept with Carmen, she didn't care what kind of issue existed between him and her father, she didn't care that he'd left her with a broken heart.

Just as before, the last time they'd made love,

all that mattered was the moment. The feel of his skin, the smell of his body, the touch of his hands.

He picked her up and carried her to the rear of the condo, to the bedroom she'd passed through earlier. It was lined with a bank of windows and they looked out over the Gulf. The water was so black and endless she couldn't tell where the glass stopped and empty space began. A storm of vertigo came over her at the sight, and Andres's touch only added to the sensation. He peeled back the robe that she wore, then dropped it to the floor, his own clothes quickly following as dizziness took hold of her.

They swayed in the darkness for one long moment. Not touching. Not breathing. Simply staring at each other, a heartbeat's distance apart. She wondered if he could tell what she was thinking—that none of their past ever mattered during a moment like this—then she knew that thought wasn't important, either. Andres was Andres and she would always love him. It was her destiny to have him in her heart.

He reached out and brushed the edge of her jaw. His touch left a path of heat all the way down her cheek to her lips. She turned her head and took his thumb into her mouth, sucking gently. His eyes burned in the darkness; she could feel their energy and taste his desire.

"You love me," he whispered. Pulling his thumb away, he rubbed it over her lips, then glided his nail over her mouth. The edge felt sharp and it escalated her desire.

She nodded slowly.

"Tell me," he demanded. "Say the words. Let me hear them come from your mouth."

She stood quietly for a moment. When she did speak, her voice was so strained, it didn't even sound like her. "I love you." Another woman *was* speaking, she thought in a daze. How on earth could she—Lena—be telling Andres she loved him? It didn't make sense.

"Show me," he demanded. "Make me believe it."

Without hesitation, she reached for him. The kiss lasted forever, then she dropped her mouth to his shoulder, then his chest, then finally lower. A few minutes later, he gasped and brought her to her feet. "If you keep doing that, I'm not going to last too long."

"How long you last isn't important." Her eyes met his in the darkness. "What counts is what you do with the time you've got."

"Then let's not waste any more of it."

CHAPTER TWELVE

WHEN LENA WOKE in the early dawn, Andres was still beside her. Gently, she touched his shoulder. As always, his lovemaking had left her both drained and fulfilled.

He stirred under her fingertips, and she realized he'd been awake all along. Turning his head against the pillow, he looked at her. "I love you," he said simply.

She closed her eyes against the feeling that came over her at his words, but the emotion was too strong to fight. All at once she was back where she'd been before, imagining life with Andres, a family, a home.

Everything she'd always wanted with the man she'd always loved.

She continued to fight the images just as she had ever since he'd left her, but they managed to get past her defenses and slip into her heart.

The bed shifted and she opened her eyes. Andres was watching her, his head propped up by one hand, his expression barely visible in the darkness of the room. He touched her face with a gentle caress. "Lena…"

Her name always sounded different coming from his lips.

"Andres…"

He smiled and let his hand drop to the tops of her breasts. Raking a fingernail across her skin, he sent shivers up and down her spine.

"You're so beautiful," he said. "So perfect."

She laughed lightly. "Me? Perfect? I don't think so, but I love to hear it. Tell me more."

"Why tell you?" He bent his head and dropped a kiss where his touch had been a second before. "When I can show you instead?"

"I have to go to work in a bit," she protested. "And I didn't sleep at all."

"You slept at least an hour."

She groaned. "I need more than that, please… and it's going to be a long day. It always is after a call-out."

She felt him tense and wished immediately that she hadn't brought up the subject. It was too late though, the words had already escaped. She eased up in the bed and started toward the edge. Andres stopped her, his hand on her arm.

"Don't leave."

She couldn't resist. Allowing him to bring her closer, she relaxed against his chest and he wrapped his arms around her. Together, they stared

out over the water. The faintest line of red marked
the eastern sky.

"Lena…" He said her name again, then she felt
him hold his breath.

She waited and for some reason, held her own.

Inside the circle of his embrace, he turned her
slightly, so he could see her face. "Lena…I want
to ask you something. Something very important.
But I don't want you to answer me, okay? I want
you to think about what I'm going to say then,
later, I will ask you again. You can tell me your
reply at that point. ¿Está bien?"

"This sounds scary." Trying to keep her voice
light, she laughed nervously. "I don't know if I
like the rules, either."

He smiled, but his eyes were serious as they
caressed her face. "Just don't answer now, that's
all I ask."

"Okay, okay…" She nodded her acceptance.

He took her hands between his and lifted them
to his mouth where he kissed her fingertips, one
by one. For a moment, he stayed quiet, as if he
were gathering his thoughts, then he raised his gaze
and spoke over the top of their joined hands. "I
love you, Lena, and returning to Destin has made
me realize that fact even though it was something
I wanted to fight at first. It's not anything that will
ever change, though. You can blame my Latin nature for saying this, but I know that we were born
to be together, no matter what. I hope that you

share these feelings with me, *querida,* and I would like to know if you would again consider marrying me.''

In the silence that suddenly filled the room, the bottom of the world fell out. Lena tumbled into the hole it left, her mouth dropping open in shock. She'd expected something important, but not this. Never this. Andres immediately reached out and covered her lips with his fingers.

''No,'' he said. ''Say nothing now. I want you to let out your feelings, allow your emotions to decide this one for you. I know we have some problems, but they can be vanquished. We have enough love to conquer them and anything else that might come our way.'' He cupped her chin with his fingers. ''I thought I could live without you, but the truth is, I can't. I love you and you love me. You said so last night. If we share that, surely we can work out our problems, no?''

''Andres, I—''

He kissed her into silence.

When he finished, he put his finger over her mouth once more. ''For once, please, just listen to what's in your heart, *querida.* Don't think—just hear what your heart says—it will tell you what to do.''

ANDRES GOT DRESSED and left a little while later. In his pale-blue robe, with her hair blowing in the early dawn's breeze, Lena stood at the front door and watched him walk to the elevators. He came back twice and kissed her each time, loath to have her out of his arms, then finally he left, driving away in his SUV, which had been delivered the night before. Both of them were reluctant to lose sight of the other, but neither had known what to do after his proposal. Especially Lena. Her eyes couldn't have gotten any larger or her body any more tense. Clearly he'd shocked her.

Which was all right. He'd shocked himself as well.

Leaving the complex, he rolled the truth over in his mind, the truth he'd come to accept some time during the night. He would never stop loving Lena, no matter what. The situation with her father, the details behind the wedding that had never happened, even Carmen's death—they were all tragedies, yes, but the truth couldn't be denied. They *were* meant for each other.

He reached the main highway in a few minutes and headed straight for the hotel where Isabel was staying. He'd called her last night with an apology for leaving her at the McKinney house, but had told her little else. Now she had to hear the grim truth about Carmen, and he wanted it to come from him, not some newscaster. Knocking on the hotel door, he waited for her to answer.

Fully dressed, Isabel opened the door a second later, a mug of steaming coffee in her hand. His aunt looked surprised but pleased to see him. "Andres! So early.... Come in, *por favor,* come in."

He stepped inside and kissed her smooth cheek. Her skin was fragrant with lavender, the scent she always wore. "I'm sorry to bother you like this even before breakfast, but—"

"No, no, it doesn't matter." She went to the minikitchen in one corner of the room, poured another cup of the strong black brew and brought it back to him. Their eyes met as she handed him the china mug, and this time she saw the darkness in his gaze.

"What's wrong?" she asked immediately.

He didn't mince words; his aunt was a strong woman. "It's Carmen San Vicente," he said. "There was a terrible accident last night."

Isabel put her hand to her chest. "Oh, no. Is she hurt?"

"She's dead, *Tia.* I'm sorry."

"Oh, no...oh, dear..." Crossing herself, she sat down on the edge of the bed. "What happened?"

He gave her the basic details, leaving out the worst of it. "We don't have an ID on the killer yet."

"Do her children know?"

"I called her father last night."

"Oh, those poor babies."

He let her talk a little more, then he asked the question that had been on his mind since talking with Phillip. "*Tia*, do you know much about Carmen's family back in Cuba?"

"I knew them well."

"Tell me what you know, please."

She didn't ask him why, she simply began to talk. Twenty minutes later, he was more confused than before. If there was anything—anything at all—in Carmen's past that might make her a friend of the Red Tide, Andres had no idea what it might be. Maybe she simply hadn't had time to tell him about the lead yet. Maybe he was looking for what wasn't there.

Then why had they killed her?

The answer to his question came so swiftly he knew it had been there all along. He'd never *really* suspected her. Carmen had been killed for asking about things she shouldn't have. They'd *had* to stop her.

Andres could think of nothing but Phillip McKinney's angry expression the day before.

Promising his aunt he'd return and take her out for lunch, Andres left the hotel and went straight to his office. Going into the small cubicle where Carmen had sat, he looked through her desk and files, but he could find nothing that looked suspicious. A quick check of her computer told him even less. If she'd made notes on her conversations with Phillip she must have kept them at home. He'd seen nothing in her condo last night, but her killer could have destroyed them. After he tortured

her to make her tell him where they were. Andres
closed his eyes against the image but that action
alone was not enough to erase the picture. He'd
seen the body.

Leaning back in the desk chair, he stared out the
window toward the parking lot, his thoughts growing cold. If Phillip had had Carmen killed, she was
his second victim. And an innocent one at that.
She'd simply gotten too close, linking Phillip to
the motel where Olvera had stayed. Was that
enough to make the old man kill her or had she
known more? It made no sense that she'd found
out something and held it back from Andres, but
he'd known of stranger things to happen during the
course of an investigation. He'd have to go back
and track down everything she'd done, repeat all
her actions. It was the only way he'd know what
she'd been doing.

LATE FRIDAY AFTERNOON, Lena finished the debriefing and dismissed the men. Their mood was
quiet, and underneath it all, she could sense the
disappointment many of them felt. She discerned
it because she felt the same way. There was no
good explanation for Carmen San Vicente's murder and the killer's identity remained a mystery.
The detectives were working on the case now, and
eventually they'd know who he was, but in the
meantime the lack of information only served to
frustrate.

Deep in thought, Lena made her way back to her office. She didn't know which was more up-setting right now—her personal life or her profes-sional one. Both were in such an uproar, she felt as if she were caught inside a tornado. Spinning and spinning, no control, no end in sight.

Andres's proposal had been so unexpected, she was still reeling. There was only one thing she was glad of and that was the fact that he hadn't wanted her to answer. She had no idea what to say, no idea what to think about the feelings storming in-side her.

Her phone was ringing as she stepped into her office.

Her father was on the other end, and Lena dropped into the chair behind her desk. This was all she needed. He was probably mad because she'd had to leave his party and wanted to let her know about it.

"Your run made the ten o'clock news." Throw-ing her off guard, his voice was subdued. "I watched it after the party. The woman who was killed, she was Andres's assistant, wasn't she?"

Lena pitched the file she'd been holding to the top of her desk. "Yes, she was. Did you know her?"

"I'd met her once." He seemed to hedge, then went on. "She was stunning."

"She *was* an attractive woman."

"Any leads yet?"

"None that I know of." Lena gripped the phone. Her father wasn't usually this attentive to her work. "Why are you so interested?"

"No particular reason," he answered quickly. "I was just surprised, that's all. Her association with Casimiro then her death. It seemed...unusual, don't you think? Did he say anything about her?"

"She was his assistant, Dad." Lena shook her head. How far would Phillip go? Did he really think he could make her believe Andres had something to do with Carmen's unfortunate murder? "He felt badly about it, of course. He said she was involved in a case he was working on, but that was all. He couldn't say more because he didn't know more. And I believe him," she added for good measure.

"Of course you would." His voice turned bitter, but instead of pursuing the issue as she would have expected, Phillip surprised her again and dropped the subject. "Did you have a good time at the party? I wish you could have stayed longer. Jeff disappeared right after you did, too. Something about a girlfriend. But he came back, at least, to take Andres's aunt home."

"I didn't finish the case until midnight, Dad," she said automatically. "The party was over by then. But I want to know what you and Andres were talking about outside on the balcony. When he came in, he looked—"

"It was business," Phillip interrupted. "A case

I've got going that the Justice Department might
impact.''

''A case?'' Her voice revealed her suspicion.

''Down in Miami,'' her father answered impatiently. ''You don't know anything about it,
Lena.''

He was lying.

As sure as she was sitting in her office, holding
the phone against her ear, he was lying. But there
was nothing she could do about it. Confronting
him would only make things worse. He'd get his
back up and she'd never find out.

What would he say if he knew of Andres's proposal?

Phillip returned to the topic of the party, and she
let him talk, her mind focusing once more on the
question that faced her. When he started to say
goodbye, she realized she hadn't heard a thing he'd
said. Which was just as well, she decided, hanging
up a second later. He'd been so imperative at the
party, she'd almost been relieved to get the call-
out. She could only imagine the blowup that would
occur should she decide to marry Andres. Did she
really want to put up with that? She twirled a pencil on her desk and shook her head. She couldn't
let her father's reaction keep her from marrying the
man she loved.

The thought startled her into stillness and she
dropped the pencil. She really did love Andres, she
realized suddenly. She'd said the words last night,

but the emotion hadn't hit her until this very moment. She *did* love him, and if that was the case, then her answer was simple, wasn't it? There was no good reason *not* to marry him. Sure, they had problems, but everyone in a relationship had problems. No one's love life was simple.

But he left you, a little voice whispered. *If he did it once, he'd do it again.*

Before she could start to argue with herself, a shadow fell over her door. Raising her eyes, she was almost grateful to see her brother standing on the threshold. The annoying voice in the back of her brain sputtered into silence. "Jeff! What are you doing here?"

"Hey, Sis." He stepped inside then took the nearest chair, dropping his briefcase to the floor as he sat down. "I had to come downtown to see a pro bono at the jail. Thought I'd stop by."

She nodded approvingly. Jeff was the only one of her brothers who took not-for-profit cases. Phillip grumbled every time Jeff handled one of the nonpaying clients, especially the criminal ones. The McKinney law firm wasn't a charity agency, he would say. Someone has to help people with no money, Jeff would always reply.

"I just talked to Dad," she said, grimacing. "He's on a tear, as usual."

"About what?"

"You name it. The party, us, Andres...I should blame his bad mood on you. It was your idea to bring Andres to the party. Where was the bad choice you threatened to show up with?"

He grinned. "I chickened out. Your inviting Andres created enough of a stir, anyway. Was the old man upset about anything else?"

"Other than Andres, not really," she said. "Same-old, same-old. You know how it is."

"I'm afraid I do." He shifted in the chair. "Tell me about the call-out. I heard some of it on the news. The woman was Andres's assistant, wasn't she?"

Lena nodded then told her brother the same thing she'd told her dad. "Andres was very upset," she added.

"I'm sure he must have been."

For a few seconds, Jeff studied her from across the desk, then he spoke. "You guys are getting serious again, aren't you?"

She kept her expression neutral. "Why do you ask?"

"I tried to call your place last night. No one answered."

"And that told you we're getting serious?"

He shook his head. "No, that told me you weren't at home, at least at 2:00 a.m. The look on your face is what told me you're getting serious."

Suddenly uncomfortable, Lena rose and stepped to the window. After a second, she turned slowly. "He's asked me to marry him."

"And your answer was?"

"I haven't given it yet."

"But you're thinking about it?"

"Yes. I am."

He stood then, too, and walked over to where she waited. She looked up at him. His eyes were blue, like Phillip's, but she couldn't read the expression in them. "I think you should say yes," he said, surprising her. "You should say yes, move to Miami with him, and have lots of babies."

She laughed suddenly.

"He loves you, Lena. He's always loved you."

"How do you know that?"

"I can just tell." He shrugged. "Don't you remember right after you got shot? I told you then that Andres loved you and you didn't believe me. Do you believe me now?"

She looked back out the window, her voice low and quiet when she spoke. "I have to, but I'm just not sure I want to."

THE BEACH WAS COLD that night, cold and lonely. From the house, Lena headed down to the dunes and past them to the shore, her feet tracing a route she'd taken a thousand times before, probably more. Ever since she'd been old enough to walk, she'd crossed these sands and gone to the water when she needed to think. And she needed that more tonight than she ever had before. She had a tremendous decision in front of her, one that would affect the rest of her life. She'd made the choice once before and been hurt so badly, it'd taken months to recover. Now she was facing it again.

She stood at the edge of the wet sand and watched the waves come in. Their white, foamy tops glowed in the dark. Flashes of silver, just beneath the surface, gave away the presence of amberjack and flounder. Over the water, as if it were scripted, a silver moon rose slowly. Its pearly reflection rippled and moved on the surface of the sea, coming in and going out with the pull of the tide.

She'd half expected Andres to show up, but after Jeff had left her office that afternoon, the rest of the day had been quiet. No one had called or stopped by. The team had been busy with training lessons and Lena had concentrated on them. Eventually, she'd gone out to the shooting range, the feel of her weapon in her hand the only thing that seemed real. She'd fired, time and time again, the targets moving, her mind whirling. When dark had slipped up on her, she'd been shocked to look down at her watch and see how much time had passed.

Now here she was. Thinking about her past and contemplating repeating it. The images of the last few weeks shot through her brain in rapid succession, each almost too vivid to bear as she relived them. Seeing Andres for the first time. Feeling the bullet hit her. Making love with him again. The look in his eyes when he'd proposed.

Everything mingled in her mind, but two thoughts stood out. She loved him. But she didn't trust him.

Lena sat down abruptly in the sand and closed her eyes for a second, her thoughts unexpectedly assailed by memories of her mother. Her death had left Lena lost. She didn't know how to act or what to do. After all, who was a child without a mother? It'd taken Lena months to learn to believe in her father. He'd been an unknown entity at the time, a shadowy figure in her life who'd been present but not really there. Forced by Dorothea's death, father and daughter had come to know each other and build the trust they'd needed. The connection between them was convoluted and not always pleasant, but Lena knew one thing for sure. Phillip had always done what he considered the best thing for her; he had her faith in that and therefore he had her love.

Trust. It was the foundation of everything.

Lena opened her eyes and stared out at the water. She'd told Andres before she didn't trust him, but until this very moment, she hadn't really thought about what that meant. Trust was what she'd had but lost when her mother died. It was the knowledge that someone would be there for you, always.

And if they weren't, there had to be a good reason—a damned good reason—for their absence.

Lena groaned in the darkness, the sudden, awful

truth so painful as it hit her she could hardly breathe. She had never believed what Andres had told her about the night he'd stood her up. She'd accepted his excuse wrapped in a fog of pain and denial, because that was the only way she could keep living. But in her heart of hearts, she'd never been sure.

If he'd lied to her and there hadn't been a special ops that night taking him from their wedding, it meant he didn't love her. If the ops *had* taken place and he'd simply chosen *not* to tell her about it, it meant he didn't trust her.

Neither choice was acceptable.

Suddenly, from somewhere down the beach, beyond where Lena sat, she heard the sound of children laughing. Staring into the darkness, her eyes adjusted and then she saw them. A family. A mom and dad with two little girls. They were flying a kite, the white triangle as pale and ephemeral as angel's wings in the inky darkness above them. Lena watched as the children jumped up and down, the strong breeze from the sea catching their long hair and whipping it into their faces. The father handed the string to the taller child. The kite dipped up and down then she passed it to the smaller one. It took a tumble before that little girl handed it back to her father who played out the line and sent it back toward the stars. He wrapped his arm around his wife while the children danced around them.

Lena stared at them and felt her heart expand. She could have this. She could have the husband, the children, even the stars above. All she had to do was reach out, take them, and bring them closer to her. All she had to do was say yes.

But she couldn't.

Not until she knew the truth.

CHAPTER THIRTEEN

IT WAS A LONG and torturous weekend, and Monday wasn't much better. The day crawled by. When six o'clock finally came, Lena was more nervous than she'd ever been in her life, but she headed straight for Andres's office. She hadn't been there before and it took longer than she expected, the traffic inching along in the early winter evening. By the time she located the building and found a parking spot, her heart felt as if were going to implode.

He was sitting at his desk, talking on the phone, when she walked inside. With an abrupt goodbye, he ended the conversation, hung up the receiver and came quickly to where she stood.

In his dark eyes she read his desire. He wanted to pull her into his arms and kiss her but he didn't know how she'd react. Obviously deciding to do what he wanted regardless, he reached out and brought her close. She didn't resist. Through the starched white shirt he wore, she could feel his warmth, his strength, and she melted against him. Their lips met in a long, deep kiss, his mouth soft but insistent against her own, his touch demanding as he pressed his case the best way he could.

It was a kiss that would have swayed any woman.

After a second, he leaned back and looked at her as she struggled with the emotions raging inside her, the ones that were tearing her in a dozen different directions.

"I've come to give you an answer." She gripped his shoulders with her hands. Beneath her fingers, his muscles were tense.

He said nothing, but he didn't need to. They each knew how important the moment was, how it would affect the rest of their lives.

She blinked, then plunged ahead.

"I want to marry you, Andres. I really do. But I have to hear the truth first. I have to know why you left me at the altar before I can make up my mind."

ANDRES STARED AT HER and tried to keep his demeanor flat and emotionless. Lena stared back. This was his worst nightmare coming to life before his eyes, but he could tell it wasn't an easy moment for her, either. Smudged beneath her eyes were dusky shadows and her mouth was outlined by tension.

"We've been over this, Lena," he said carefully. "I told you what happened when I came back and tried to reconcile with you after the wedding.''

''Tell me again.''

''I don't think this is necessary—''

''Then my answer is no.'' Her gray eyes were tortured as they met his. ''I have to be able to trust you. And I don't right now. I didn't realize how important that really is until last night, but the more I thought about it, the more I understood. I can't marry you without trusting you.''

''But I love you!'' he said. ''You love me! That's enough.''

''No, it's not. Not for me.''

His chest went tight, as if he were being pressed between two metal plates, and he took a step backward. Away from her.

''I'm afraid that history will repeat itself,'' she said sadly. ''That I'll give you my heart and you'll leave me again.''

''That won't happen.''

''How do I know for sure?''

''Because our circumstances are completely different. What happened then *can't* happen now. I've explained this already.''

''No, you didn't explain anything,'' she said. ''You gave me a tale about a special ops and told me that was all you could say.'' Her jaw tightened. ''I don't believe that's the truth—at least not all of it.''

"This is crazy," he said harshly. "Why drag this up now?"

"Look, Andres, I'm a cop. I take care of business first and worry about why later. When you left me I was so devastated I accepted what you told me because I didn't have another choice. I had to close my eyes and keep going. But you told me to feel, not to think, and your aunt said something similar at Thanksgiving. Last night I let my emotions out and for the first time I realized, deep down, what it really meant not to trust you."

She took a deep breath. "I can't pretend the past never happened. I just can't do it, not without knowing you won't leave me again. Otherwise, I'll spend the rest of my life worrying every time you walk out the door."

"Lena, I promise you—"

She shook her head and stopped him. "If what happened was a special ops, you should have explained," she said resolutely. "I would have understood the situation, no matter what. Were you afraid I'd jeopardize the mission? If you were, then—"

"That wasn't the reason. You're a good cop, Lena. One of the best I've ever known."

His compliment went ignored.

"Then if it wasn't a professional decision," she said quietly, "I can only come to one other conclusion."

He looked at her.

"You don't really love me. And you never have. You made up the story just to avoid the wedding."

"No!" He spoke with such unexpected force, she stumbled back. Reaching for her, his fingers found only air.

He dropped his outstretched hand back to his side and softened his voice. "I love you with all my heart, Lena. You are my life. You're the very reason I live. You're everything that's good and strong and perfect."

She started shaking her head before he finished. "Don't lie to me—"

"I'm not," he insisted. "I've lived through ten kinds of hell but leaving you when I did—knowing you were waiting for me at that altar when I couldn't get there—it was the worst. You *have* to believe me when I tell you that."

He heard her take a tiny breath—almost a sigh— and something unsaid passed between their hearts. He could feel it; a flutter, a warmth, a brief moment in time. The sensation might have given him hope except for her expression.

"I do believe you," she said finally. "I actually do…but that isn't enough. I have to trust that you won't leave me again after you've made me love you. And I don't. Not with what you've told me."

Andres struggled, a huge heartache building inside him. He'd never wanted Lena to have to pick between her father or him. He'd had to make that kind of gut-wrenching, life-changing decision when he'd chosen freedom over staying in Cuba, and it'd been the hardest thing he'd ever done. He'd always wanted to protect Lena from having such a dilemma.

But suddenly he realized how wrong he'd been.

He hadn't been protecting Lena—he'd been protecting himself. She would ask him for proof and he had none. She'd do what he'd always feared the most. She'd abandon him as he had her.

How could he have been so blind? He sighed heavily. "If I tell you the truth, you'll leave me."

"I'll leave you if you don't."

The words fell like stones at his feet. After a long moment, he nodded sadly and began to speak.

"WHAT I EXPLAINED before was what happened," he began, "but I didn't tell you everything."

Lena's pulse began to throb so hard at the base of her neck, she knew Andres could probably hear it, as well as see it.

"I couldn't tell you," he said, "because you wouldn't have believed me. You still won't."

"That's for me to judge."

He didn't answer her. Instead, turning away from her, he went to his desk and pulled something out. When he came back and handed a piece of paper to her, she saw it was a photograph. The tattered black-and-white snapshot showed two little boys sitting in a beat-up rowboat that was half buried in the sand. They were both dark-haired and poorly dressed, about six years old. They looked as though they didn't get enough to eat.

"That's my best friend, Mateo Aznar, in the back of the boat. And that's me, in the front."

She raised her gaze to his in surprise. She'd never seen a childhood photo of Andres. She focused once more on the picture, and the image of the little boy he'd been so long ago stole her heart. He had eyes that were way too old.

"I lied when I said the only thing I took out of Cuba was my grandfather's ring." He nodded toward the photo. "I took that snapshot, too. We were inseparable. We were like brothers. I loved him."

Her mouth filled with sand, making it hard to speak. "Loved? Past tense?"

"Mateo is dead." His eyes went flat. "He was murdered the night of the wedding."

Lena saw life and death every day, but something about the way Andres spoke now put his harsh pronouncement into a different perspective. She reached out for the chair behind her, and when her fingers felt the arms, she sank down into the seat. "What happened?"

He took the photo from her hand and walked back to his desk. Slipping it inside the center drawer as if he couldn't stand to look at it any longer, he spoke.

"After I joined Justice, Mateo helped me. He became a source of information. A spy, if you will.

He fed me everything he could about the Red Tide, and I passed it on. The day you and I were to marry he called me and told me the Tide had found out about him. They were searching for him even then, and as soon as they could find him, they were going to kill him. He was hiding, but didn't have much hope. He begged me to try a rescue.''

Andres turned his face away from Lena, his profile all lines and hard edges. ''I left the minute I could and flew to Miami to rent a boat. I went to the island that night to try to get him, but the Red Tide knew about our rendezvous. They killed him as he swam toward me.''

Stunned into silence, all Lena could do was stare. ''This was the operation you told me about, wasn't it?'' she finally asked. ''The one where you lost your friend and felt responsible for it?''

He nodded once. After a second, she spoke softly. ''Why didn't you tell me all this, Andres? My God… Surely you knew I would have understood.''

He turned slowly. ''I couldn't tell you, Lena. It was too risky.''

''Too risky?'' She stood, confusion sweeping over her. ''What do you mean? Did you think I'd tell the authorities you were going to Cuba? C'mon, Andres, it's illegal, yes, but surely you didn't think I'd—''

He shook his head. ''That's not it.''

''Then what?''

"There was someone else involved. Someone here in the States."

His voice was remote, his demeanor cold. She'd never seen him like this before. It scared her.

"I don't understand...."

"Money had been coming into the Tide in small amounts, but a larger payment was made. A payment for something specific. Mateo had proof of the payments but they went down with him." He looked at his desk as if gathering his thoughts. Or maybe his courage. When he raised his eyes, they were even colder. "We didn't know what the money was for."

Lena felt a shadow pass over her, then he spoke again. "But we knew it came from here. From Destin." He paused. "Specifically, from your father's office."

She looked at him dumbly and simply repeated his words. "My father?"

He nodded.

"What are you—" Licking her lips, she stopped and tried again. "Are you saying—"

The second time was no better. How could she ask a question when her brain couldn't process the information he was giving her?

He took pity on her and answered what she couldn't ask. "He wanted me out of your life, Lena, and he used the Red Tide to do it."

"That's insane." It was the only thing she could

say. Andres had clearly lost his mind. "My father would never do something like that."

"I know this is difficult for you to believe, Lena, but I'm telling you the truth. I wouldn't lie to you about something this important, I promise."

"Are you saying he got involved with a terrorist group just to keep you from marrying me?"

"No. I'm telling you he was involved with them all along and when it was convenient, he used them to try to get rid of me. I was getting closer to him, closer to proving my case, and he was going to have to do something soon. The night of the wedding gave him the perfect alibi. No one would be able to pin the deaths on him because he would be in Destin, and everyone would know that."

"But why? Why would he be involved with people like that? What's the motive?"

Andres shook his head. "I don't know. All I can tell you is that he has a client named Pablo Escada. Escada is into drugs and around here drugs mean the Red Tide. It's a connection, that's all I can say. I can't explain more. Only your father can do that."

She shook her head.

"Mateo wasn't the only one under fire that night. The men who shot him tried for me, too. I was wounded, but I made it back to Miami."

"This is outrageous," she countered hotly. "Where's your proof?"

"I told you—Mateo was bringing out records

that he felt would seal the case, but they went down with him. I couldn't recover his body.''

He looked at her steadily. "After I came back I investigated your father for months. There was nothing to link him and the Red Tide but Escada. I hate Phillip, Lena, but I'm not an idiot. I wasn't going to bring charges if I couldn't back them up.''

She felt a small tick of confusion. She'd heard cops recount stories a thousand times and the way Andres was talking, the way he was presenting the facts, felt so right, it was scary. That wasn't enough, though. She couldn't believe him based on that—not when everything else sounded so bizarre. ''I can't believe this, Andres—''

''I know.'' He spoke simply. ''I didn't want to tell you before because I was afraid it'd make you crazy, that'd you'd be torn between believing me and listening to your father. Then I realized the truth. You're Phillip's daughter, yes, but you think like a cop. You'd look for evidence and look for proof.'' He held out his hands. ''And I had none…''

His words died, and she understood immediately what that meant. "But you think you've got some now,'' she said incredulously.

''It's what Carmen was working on. I believe she might have found a link between Phillip and Esteban Olvera.''

Shaking her head, Lena wanted to cry, but she wouldn't allow herself the luxury. Her throat stung with the effort. "You're kidding yourself, Andres. My father would never put me in any kind of danger—"

"Your getting shot was an accident, Lena. That sniper was aiming for me."

"Of course he was! And there's no way in hell you can tie my father to him, either."

He stepped closer and started talking about a car. She let him speak, her mind catching the details, but refusing to accept them. "Save your breath," she said finally, interrupting him. "This is just crazy. Absolutely crazy."

He fell silent and they stared at each other. After one long heartbeat, Lena realized there were no more words between them. There was no more… anything.

She turned and walked to the door of his office. As her fingertips closed around the doorknob, she knew she had to ask one last question even though she knew the answer would be a deception, like everything else had been. Pivoting slowly, she let her eyes meet his for the last time.

"How could you do this to me?" she said quietly. "How could you come back here and make me fall in love with you all over again—knowing this lie was between us?"

She was afraid he might cross the room, that he might come to where she was and try to convince her with his mouth, his arms, his eyes. But he made no attempt to move. In the end, she realized he

didn't need to touch her. She could feel the force
of his words, of his truth, from across the room. It
hit her with a strength that almost made her sway.

"I love you," he said simply. "I've never
stopped loving you. Nothing means more than
that."

She wanted to believe him so badly, she felt ill
with the need inside her.

Instead she opened the door and left.

LENA DROVE directly to Phillip's office, but by the
time she got there, the windows were dark and the
building was closed. There was no one inside.

She got out of her car anyway and strode up to
the etched-glass doors. She wanted the facts and
she wanted them now. There was too much at stake
to wait. Raising her fists, she pounded on the heavy
glass. She wanted to smash the glass—to smash
something—into as many tiny pieces as her life
was in at this moment. The doors didn't move, of
course, and nothing even remotely dramatic happened. After a second, she stepped to the side and
beat on the windows but the building stubbornly
remained dark and no one responded.

She wanted to cry, but she'd been holding in her
tears since she was nine years old. What good
would it serve to let them out now? She walked
back to her vehicle, her heart bruised and heavy.

Inside the truck she started the engine, but before she could reverse out of the parking space, a

sudden thump at the back of the vehicle made her slam on the brakes. Wincing, she swung her head around to see Bering standing beside the curb. Huffing from the jog he'd made between the office and the parking lot, he'd obviously slammed the fender with his fist to get her attention.

"Oh, shit..." He was all she needed right now.

His face red, his eyebrows woven into an angry scowl, her brother rounded the vehicle to stand beside her door. He was talking before she could even lower the window.

"What on earth are you doing, Lena? I saw you from the window upstairs. I had clients in my office, for God's sake! I had to take them out the back so they wouldn't see my sister acting like a crazy person on the front steps."

Any of her other brothers, especially Jeff, would have asked what was wrong. Not Bering. "I'm looking for Dad," she answered stonily.

"Well, he's not here. He's in Atlanta. He's on a case over there."

She nodded and put the truck back into reverse, then suddenly she had another thought. She braked and looked at her brother. "I need to know something. About the firm."

"What?" he asked suspiciously.

"Do you represent a guy named Escada? First name, Pablo?"

His expression immediately froze. "Why do you want to know that?"

"It's important," she answered. "Just tell me—"

"I can't. That's privileged information—"

"Oh, for God's sake, Bering, get real! I can look up the goddamn case myself tomorrow morning when the courthouse opens, but I need to know right now! Did the firm represent him or not?"

"Don't you curse at me, Lena Marie." He pursed his mouth tightly, and she knew she had lost. "I'm not telling you a thing. You're a cop! You should know better than to even ask. Wait until morning and find out for yourself!"

She started to ask him more, but he made a huffing sound of disapproval then headed toward the office. He was moving quicker than he'd been when he'd come out to the car. When he got to the sidewalk, he shot a quick glance over his shoulder then scuttled back into the office. She cursed again. Why had she even tried?

She made the trip home without even thinking about what she was doing. She was almost startled when she realized she was in front of her drive. Turning into the curved shell road, she parked the truck and killed the motor. The resulting quiet was unbroken and complete, the only sound she could hear was the roar of the waves coming from behind the house. With leaden feet, she went inside.

The phone rang just as she opened the front door. Thinking it might be Sarah, Lena threw her bag to the table in the entry, hurrying into the living room. She grabbed it on the third ring.

"Lena, sweetheart, it's Isabel. Can you talk with an old lady for a few moments?"

Dropping to her sofa, Lena closed her eyes and rubbed them, gripping the phone. "Of course, I have time for you, Isabel. I'm not too sure you'll want to talk to me, though. It hasn't been a good day."

"I'm sorry to hear that." Isabel's voice was soothing and kind, a lilting balm to Lena's frazzled soul. "Tell me about it. What made it so bad?"

The urge to unload, to cry and to let out all her raw emotions was overwhelming and almost too big to fight. Lena struggled with the yearning and finally managed to get herself under control. What good would it be to tell Isabel everything? She loved her nephew like the son he almost was to her; he'd be the one she'd defend and understand.

Lena opened her eyes. Maybe he'd already called Isabel. Maybe that was why she was calling Lena.

"Andres and I had a fight," Lena said cautiously. "Do you know about it?"

"Oh, dear...oh, dear..."

Lena knew immediately Isabel hadn't spoken to Andres.

"No, no. I know nothing. I simply called to chat. What happened?"

"He asked me to marry him—"

"Oh, *Dios mío*…"

"And I turned him down."

It was Isabel's turn to be silent, and Lena could only imagine the thoughts spinning through the older woman's head.

"I am very sorry to hear this," she said finally. "I love you, Lena, and having you in our family would make me very happy. If it isn't meant to be, though, it's not meant to be."

Lena's throat closed. It took her a moment to speak. "I'm flattered that you feel that way. I think a lot of you, as well. Unfortunately, though…there are problems. Problems I don't know how to deal with."

"Is there anything I can do, or would I just be an old woman meddling?"

Lena shook her head, even though, of course, Andres's aunt couldn't see her. "You would never be a meddler. But I'm afraid there's nothing anyone can do. Andres has said some things, made some accusations, that I simply can't accept. About my family."

"I'm so sorry."

"I am, too." Lena looked out the bank of windows that made up her living room wall. An empty blackness, as stark and desolate as her future, stretched beyond the other side of the glass. No husband. No lover. No children.

"Would it make a difference if I told you how much he loves you?"

"There's too much between us now, too much that's not good. The things he said were—" She stopped, her throat going tight.

"Oh, Lena...our hearts aren't always connected to the rest of our body, you know."

"Wh-what do you mean?"

"Your heart...your brain... You and Andres react so differently. He feels first and then thinks. You think first and then decide if you can feel. It's just like Yolanda and Angelo."

Lena and Isabel had discussed Andres's parents only last week but it seemed as if it'd happened a year ago. "I hear what you're saying, Isabel, but this time I think you're wrong. I am feeling this with my heart. And that's the problem. And I simply can't accept what he had to say. The emotions are there—but the facts aren't."

"Is that so important?"

"Facts are the only thing we have to go on, Isabel. There isn't another way, no matter how I feel." As she spoke, she got the sudden feeling that Isabel knew exactly what they were talking about. Andres had told the older woman his suspicions of Phillip.

"I understand, *chica*. You have to live your way. We all do. Remember this, though..." There was silence on the other end of the phone. "Andres loves you very, very much. He wouldn't have said what he did unless he had good reason. You might want to think about that and ask yourself what that would be."

CHAPTER FOURTEEN

ANDRES LOST the rest of the week. He ate when he was supposed to, worked at what was before him, went to bed when the clock struck midnight. None of the activities registered, though. He was merely going through the motions of living, a paralyzing numbness taking over because he couldn't bear to face what had actually happened.

His aunt's telephone call caught him at his desk on Friday evening.

"I'm worried about you," she said. "I think you should come home." They'd talked once briefly and he'd told her about Lena. Isabel had been sympathetic but beneath her words there had been a kind of unspoken censure he wasn't sure he understood.

"I can't," he replied without thinking. "I have work to do."

"And are you really doing it or just sitting there, staring out the window?"

He blinked as her words hit their mark.

"Come home," she said, not waiting for his answer. "Come just for the weekend if nothing else and we can talk."

He refused once again and they spoke for a little while more, but by the time he got ready for bed, Andres decided Isabel might be right. Some time away from Destin, away from the presence of Lena's ghost in his bed, was probably a very good idea. He reached for the phone on the nightstand and called the airline, booking a flight for the next day. There was no real need for him to stay in Destin Saturday and Sunday, and he'd made so little progress in trying to figure out what Carmen had been doing that it was depressing.

Maybe his heart wouldn't be so numb in Miami.

He turned out the light and lay down on the bed, feeling the lie crumble as the darkness came over him. He would feel the same no matter where he was, and he knew it as surely as he knew the sun would come up tomorrow. He was incapable of hearing anything but the truth since he'd realized his denial about Lena. Without it to protect him, he couldn't deceive himself about anything anymore.

In the days since their confrontation, truth after truth had descended on him. He'd had no idea how much he'd depended on something other than reality to sustain him.

He'd always thought he could make Lena love him again.

He'd always thought they'd marry.

He'd always thought Phillip McKinney was guilty of murder.

How many of those *facts* weren't real? Like the other certainties he'd realized were false, Andres couldn't bear to consider the answer.

He went to sleep and dreamed of Lena.

LENA WOKE UP Saturday morning, rolled over in the bed and covered her head with the pillow. It'd been a helluva week—a nightmare of a week—and she really wished she could just lie there and sleep until it was all over. The only problem was she was afraid it would never be all over. She couldn't stop thinking about Andres's accusation against her father. It had consumed her. She'd returned to Phillip's office Tuesday but Reba had confirmed Bering's information, saying Phillip wouldn't be back for at least two weeks. Lena had considered calling him, but this wasn't exactly something that could be discussed over the phone, especially since she knew Phillip would go ballistic. Bering's evasiveness had bothered her the more she'd thought about it, too. What did he know about the situation he wasn't telling her?

And if all that wasn't enough, Isabel's words continued to haunt Lena. When he'd been on the force, Andres had been an excellent policeman, and his hunches were usually good ones. He was emotional, yes, and depended more on his instincts than Lena ever would, but he wasn't a man who jumped to conclusions. If she thought about it logically she had to admit he wouldn't have felt the way he did about Phillip unless he'd had good reason.

But he had no proof.

Lena went round and round in her thinking, but she kept returning to the very same points. Phillip could be obnoxious and pompous but he wasn't a criminal. She remembered some of the men who'd come to their home, before Phillip had become so successful, when she was just a kid. They claimed to be his friends from college who jokingly said he'd sold out as he made more and more money. But to think he'd support a terrorist organization was simply bizarre.

Lena made a vow. Monday morning, she'd start her own investigation. She'd get someone discreet working on it, maybe Sarah. There were too many questions in the air, too much chaos. Andres hadn't found the truth, but maybe he didn't know where to look. He was investigating *her* family, after all. She should know where the skeletons were, right?

Feeling slightly better with a decision made, Lena climbed out of the tangled blankets to stumble into the bathroom and wash her face. In exactly one hour she had to be at the range. She was supervising a training exercise for a small police team from Alabama. They wanted to start a multicounty SWAT team like the Emerald Coast's and needed to know more about the requirements. Lena frequently ran classes like this and usually she enjoyed them. Today that wouldn't be the case.

She was on-site twenty minutes later. Beck had volunteered to help, and he was setting up a table of weapons as she pulled up, his white-blond hair shining in the sun.

"You look like hell," he said as a way of greeting her.

"Thanks for the compliment." Lena looked over her sunglasses and braced herself for more.

It didn't come. Instead, he nodded toward the other end of the firing range from where they stood. "You have a visitor."

Automatically assuming it was Andres, Lena caught her breath and whirled around. But instead of Andres, her father waited. He stood off to one side, near one of the picnic tables under the trees. He looked thin, Lena thought with a start, thin and old.

"He was out there when I arrived." Beck ran an oiled rag over the barrel of the gun he was cleaning. "Said he'd called the station, and they'd told him you were coming here this morning."

"That's strange...." Lena shook her head. "I thought he was in Atlanta. I guess Reba told him I was looking for him, but why didn't he just go to the house?"

Beck shrugged. "Can't answer that. He does seem a little preoccupied."

Feeling uneasy, Lena headed toward her father.

She called out as she neared and he looked up and waved.

It was a halfhearted gesture and only served to increase her anxiousness. She reached the shady spot a few seconds later. "Did you get my message?" Not waiting for an answer, she continued. "I want to talk to—"

"Whatever it is, it's going to have to wait." His voice was gruff. He looked so exhausted he almost seemed ill. "I've got something I want to tell you first."

She felt an alarm go off inside her. "Are you all right? What's wrong?"

"What makes you think anything's wrong?"

"Well, you could have just called me, for one thing," she said. "And for another, you're supposed to be in Atlanta."

"Bering called and told me you were looking for me. I decided I'd better get back."

"Why?"

"I wanted to see you."

"Here?"

"I wanted neutral ground. It's always a better place for confessions."

Before she could react to the startling word, Phillip reached over and took her hand. Following her mother's death, Lena had sorely missed the physical closeness she'd shared with Dorothea. Each time she'd tried to climb into her father's lap or hold his hand, he'd gently, but firmly, pushed

her away. She'd finally learned not to even ask for
it. Only in the past few years had he managed to
bestow the occasional affectionate gesture. But his
touch felt ominous now, and she almost winced.

Moving to the table, he pulled her with him. He
sat down on one side and she took the other, his
eyes bright and steady as they met hers. "I want
to tell you about something that I did. A while
back."

Her pulse jumped.

"I'm not proud of what I did, but for the thou-
sandth time Reba has pointed out to me that you're
a grown woman. She called me an old fool and
told me she wouldn't have anything else to do with
me if I didn't tell you the truth."

Lena felt a tiny shock wave break over her at
the way he spoke about his secretary. Her mind
continued to spin but it landed on this inconse-
quential detail. It almost seemed as if she couldn't
bear to focus on the important part.

"Why would you listen to Reba when you've
never listened to me?"

"She's been with me a very long time," he answered carefully. "Reba and I have grown...close
over the years. I respect her advice." He shook his
head almost ruefully. "Actually, I *have* to—she's
relentless if I don't."

Lena stared at him in amazement. "You mean
you and Reba..."

He looked at her with wry amusement. "I may

be old, Lena, but I'm not dead." His voice dropped. "Reba's a beautiful woman, inside and out. And I was only forty-five when your mother died. I didn't want to be alone forever."

When Dorothea had passed away, he'd only been ten years older than Lena was right now. Surprised, she said, "I never thought about it before...."

"That's because I didn't want you to," he told her stoically. "I could never have replaced your mother, and I didn't want you kids to have to adjust to another woman in the house just because I needed someone. Reba understood. The arrangement fit her fine." He glanced down at his left hand and twisted the gold band he'd always worn. Lena realized she'd never wondered about that, either.

Phillip looked up from his wedding ring. "I didn't come here to discuss Reba, Lena. I came here to tell you something else."

Beneath the table, she laced her fingers nervously. Her mouth was too dry to even swallow.

He spoke without preliminary. "I came to tell you that I tried to bribe Andres to leave you when you two were about to marry. I offered him half a million dollars to walk away from you and never come back to Destin."

After the few days she'd just had, Lena wouldn't have thought it possible for her to experience another shock. *Wrong.*

"You what?"

"I offered him money not to marry you." He held his hands out over the table, then dropped them. "He turned me down. Then he walked away. I was so happy to see the last of him I didn't give a damn why he did what he did, but that doesn't make what I did any less wrong. I shouldn't have done it and I'm asking you to forgive me."

Lena let the words roll over her. Then she attempted to connect the accusations Andres had made with this latest news, but the two wouldn't come together.

"You offered him money," she said slowly, "to leave me...."

"I thought I was protecting you, Lena. I thought Andres wasn't the man for you and I wanted him out of your life any way I could arrange it. As I said, I'm not proud of what I did, but I did it out of love."

All she could think was one thing: what if Andres had told her the truth? She swallowed hard as the thought played out to its logical end. Was Phillip telling her this now because he had more to confess? She started to ask him directly, then thought again. Direct wasn't the best way to deal with her father.

Especially, a little voice in the back of her head whispered, *if Andres is right.*

"And you're telling me this because Reba wanted you to?" she asked slowly.

He seemed hesitant, but he answered, "I'm telling you this because it's haunting me, and Reba knows how badly. She's worried about my health. When you got shot, it nearly killed me, Lena, but it made me realize life is too short for the foolishness of lies. I would have never forgiven myself if you'd been hurt more seriously...or worse."

She licked her lips. "But the shooting wasn't your fault...."

"Of course not! But what I did was wrong. I tried to get Andres to leave you and he did. Whether or not I was responsible for his departure is beside the point. The result was the same...your heart was broken."

"Oh, Dad..." Lena looked above her father's head. She blinked several times, then met his gaze. She knew instinctively he was telling her the truth.

Still she had to pursue it. She was, after all, a cop. She framed her question as carefully as she could. "After you offered him the money and he turned it down, did you try any other way to get Andres out of my life?"

A line formed between his silver eyebrows. He was clearly puzzled. "I didn't have to. He never showed up at the wedding and that was that."

"Are you sure?"

"Of course I'm sure." He looked at her with some of his old impatience. "What are you implying?"

"I'm not implying anything. But a few days ago, Andres asked me to marry him."

She had to give him credit. Phillip didn't react at all. He simply stared at her.

"I told him no," she said. "Not unless he explained why he stood me up."

His eyes went wary. "And did he?"

"He told me he had to go back to Cuba to rescue a friend. The friend was killed, though. By the Red Tide."

She told herself she didn't see it, but it seemed as though Phillip blanched.

"Tell me more."

She gave him as few of the details as she could. She couldn't come right out and reveal Andres suspected him—to say that much went totally against her training as a cop, but she told him what she could. As she talked, she studied his face. He absorbed each point as if preparing for a case. He didn't seemed surprised by anything she told him, and a heavy coldness settled over her, despite the morning sunshine.

She finished her brief explanation. Phillip didn't move, but something in his expression changed and she knew before he spoke he had figured it out. He knew exactly what she *hadn't* said: that Andres believed Phillip was the man behind everything.

"And did Andres say who supposedly funded

all this? Terrorism doesn't come cheap, you know.''

"He said the money came from the States," she hedged.

His face stayed as smooth as the table between them. "Did he have proof?"

"His proof went down with his friend. At the time, it was all he had."

"At *the time*. Are you saying—"

"He's found another link."

Phillip's eyes jerked to her face.

"He thinks there's a local tie to Olvera," she said. "The man who tried to kill me."

Her father closed his eyes and stayed motionless for several long moments. Finally he opened his eyes and locked them on her face. When he spoke, his voice was strained in a way she'd never heard before.

"I didn't want Andres in your life, Lena. I thought I knew what was best for you, and it wasn't him."

A giant hand began to squeeze her throat.

"But I didn't do what he obviously thinks. I swear to you on your mother's grave. I didn't set up the attempt on his life. And I would never, ever do something to endanger you. I love you."

Lena was sitting down, but she still went weak. "Then who did? Who paid the Red Tide back then? Who's paying them now?"

His jaw tightened, then he relaxed it, so deliberately she could see the muscles move. "I have no idea."

She looked at him sharply. She didn't like the way he spoke and her suspicions rose. "Are you sure—"

As if propelled by an unseen hand, he stood suddenly, his expression imperious, his attitude defensive. "Of course, I'm sure. Andres is simply trying to discredit me. But he's way off-base."

She opened her mouth to reply, but fell silent as he rounded the table to come to her side.

"God, I'm sorry, baby." He dropped both his hands on her shoulders. "I'm sorry. All I ever wanted was to be a good father—to you and your brothers—but I've screwed it up royally. Your mother is probably standing in heaven shaking her fist at me."

Lena met her father's regretful stare, the complex, confusing nature of their relationship coming sharply into focus once more. How could she love him *and* hate him at the very same time? She couldn't answer, but she knew one thing: she couldn't be mad at him. Not now. Somewhere in the telling of the story, she'd seen the man he really was. Lonely. Worried. Doing the best he could. How could she blame him for what he'd done? It'd had no impact on Andres's decision anyway.

Feeling even more adrift than ever before, Lena

put her arms around her father and hugged him for a long time.

THE MIAMI AIRPORT was as bright and colorful as always but Andres walked down the corridor in a fog, not seeing the overhead replica of the Wright Brothers' airplane, not hearing the dozens of Spanish dialects, not even noticing the ever present drug dogs and their handlers.

He grabbed a taxi and went directly home. His house felt empty and smelled stale. The lone ivy his aunt had insisted on giving him had died a slow death, its leaves now brown and shriveled. He clicked on the air-conditioning and then the television but the emptiness was overwhelming. He'd gotten accustomed to the sound of the waves back in Destin and the silence here was simply too thick. Unable to bear it, he took a quick shower, called Isabel, and headed for her high-rise.

She met him at the door with a kiss, then led him through the small condo to her balcony. The whole place was redolent with mouthwatering smells wafting out from the kitchen. Andres recognized the main one—she was cooking *lechón asado*—a classic Cuban dish of shredded pork with lemon and garlic. Underneath that aroma, he caught a whiff of cilantro and black beans. She'd made all his favorites. For dessert there would be flan and hot Cuban coffee, served in tiny cups that were hardly needed. The bitter brew was so strong it could stand by itself.

They reached the balcony and Isabel slid back the doors. She was on the fourteenth floor and Biscayne Bay shimmered in the distance, the evening sunlight cutting diamonds on the bright-blue water. As he settled into a patio chair, she poured him a drink from a pitcher sitting on a nearby silver tray. Bacardi, mango and pineapple juice with just a hint of dry vermouth. The drink went down easily and she refilled his glass a moment later.

They sat in silence for a while and let the alcohol do its job.

After a bit, he spoke.

"She won't talk to me." He didn't have to say Lena's name. They both understood. "I've tried to call her several times and I went back to the house twice. She wouldn't come to the door."

"Did you expect something different?" Isabel spoke in Spanish. The words sounded less harsh but their meaning wasn't.

"No," he said. Holding his aunt's crystal goblet up to the dying light, he shook his head. "I suppose I didn't."

"You hurt her. Again."

"She wanted the truth."

"Of course she did. Any woman would. You should have given it to her the minute you came back from Havana."

"You know I couldn't do that. It would have totally jeopardized my investigation."

"But you did it now."

"I had to," he answered. "And it hardly matters anyway. The case is going nowhere."

She looked over at him, her eyebrows rising in surprise. "But you told me Carmen had linked Phillip—"

"Apparently she did. I can't duplicate her steps, though, and without solid proof…" His frustration boiled over and he cursed soundly. "I can't believe it, *Tia!* I *know* Phillip McKinney is behind this— I know it! Yet everywhere I turn, I reach a dead end."

"Maybe you're trying *too* hard. Sometimes the answer is obvious, but when you get too wrapped up you can't see it."

He shook his head. "Not possible."

"But Lena loves you. Knowing that should make anything possible."

"I thought it would—that's why I asked her to marry me—but I'm not so sure anymore. About that and a lot of other things as well."

"Lena's love for you is something she can't shed. It's like her skin." His aunt drilled him with a stern, unforgiving stare. "It's the same for you. You may live to be a hundred, but you will never forget her, no matter what."

His aunt's words disturbed him, and Andres turned the conversation in a different direction after that. Ordinarily stubborn about such things, she seemed to sense his need and allowed him to fill the rest of the evening with idle talk. They lingered for a long time over their meal, the food as filling and rich as the smells that had greeted Andres when he'd first arrived. Finally, after he dried the last gold-edged coffee cup and put it in the cabinet, he turned to his aunt and gently gathered her into his arms. Her frailty always surprised him when he hugged her; her strength was so tangible he forgot it wasn't physical as well.

She smiled up at him. *"Te amo, chico...."*

"I love you, too, *Tia*." Switching to Spanish as well, he smiled down at her, thinking how lucky he was to have someone like her. Their relationship was a special one. "Thank you for listening to my problems this evening. Do they make you weary?"

She reached up and patted his cheek. "No, no. Of course not. I'm worried about you, though."

"Don't be. I'll work it out somehow."

"And Lena? Will she work it out, *también?*"

"I don't know." He heard the sadness in his voice and didn't bother to hide it. "I'm afraid we may never be together."

"It would be a shame to waste the love you both share. It's too rare for that."

"I know, but I've broken her heart too many times. I wouldn't be the man I am unless I did what I've done, though. I've spent all my life protecting people, trying to do the right thing." He paused. "To live as you raised me."

"Are there no exceptions?"

"If Lena's father is a criminal, I can't look the other way."

"Even if it means sacrificing your love for her?"

His gaze went over his aunt's head, to the window and the darkness beyond. Somewhere out there, Lena was as angry and confused as he was, and neither had the power to make those feelings go away.

He thought about the issues all the way back to Destin the following day, but the truth stayed the same, and so did he.

CHAPTER FIFTEEN

ANDRES WENT STRAIGHT from the tiny Destin airport to his office Sunday night. There was nothing waiting for him at the condo. He might as well get some work done.

He dropped his briefcase at the table where Carmen had worked, then he walked toward the back, to his private area. But he stopped midway and turned to look at the empty chair. In Miami, he'd visited Carmen's family. Her children, a boy, five, and a girl, seven, had been quiet and subdued as Andres had talked with their grandfather. They were beautiful kids and they'd studied him silently with huge brown eyes identical to Carmen's. In their stillness he'd sensed their pain and confusion. Their mother was gone and no one could change that. Luis, Carmen's father, had cried when Andres had handed him the small box of things he'd gathered from Carmen's desk. The rest of her belongings, from her rented apartment, would be shipped, he'd told the older man, but Andres had brought some items she'd obviously cared about. A snapshot of her father and the children. A rosary. A birthday card she'd bought for one of the children but hadn't had time to mail.

Andres had escaped as soon as he could.

Retracing his steps, he returned to Carmen's space and sat down. He'd gone through everything too many times to count, but he'd found absolutely no clues of what she was doing or why. Despite his earlier efforts, Andres let his brain drift over the well-worn path one more time.

Carmen had traced the silver car that had been seen at Olvera's motel to AAA Bail Bonds.

Phillip McKinney owned AAA Bail Bonds.

All the employees who had access to the car had rock-solid alibis as did Phillip himself. Andres had verified that fact with Jeff as soon as he could following Carmen's death. Jeff hadn't asked any questions in return, either. He was the kind of lawyer who knew that sometimes it was better *not* to know more.

But Andres couldn't shake the idea that he was missing something obvious. When he figured out who had been behind that wheel, he would know who'd hired Olvera. It was just that simple.

It was just that difficult.

He worked at Carmen's desk, lost in thought, for two more hours. Finally, scribbling on a yellow pad she'd left in her center desk drawer, he began to take inventory of the points he knew for sure. Not his suppositions, not his feelings, nothing but the facts. Phillip's association to the bail bond company. His ties to Pablo Escada. The past in all its stark detail. Andres compiled the list then drew the lines to connect the names and times.

The process was similar to one he'd experienced when he'd looked at a hidden image in a puzzle book once. The abstract drawing had been made of squares and diamonds, but as he'd stared, something else had made itself visible. Slowly, almost maddeningly, a second image began to emerge here as well. The picture wasn't one Andres could even recognize at first and then, as it became more visible, he refused to even consider it. The closer he looked, though, the more clear it became. He couldn't deny it. No one could.

His mind reeling with the revelation, he threw his notes into his briefcase, hastily locked the office and ran outside. He had to find Lena. That was all he could think.

He had to find Lena.

SUNDAY NIGHT came too fast. Lena needed more time on the beach, more time by herself, more time period…to think about everything that had happened. Her father's admission about his attempt to bribe Andres was something she was still trying to absorb. Had Phillip really thought Andres would take money to leave her? He should have known better if he had.

Getting ready for bed that night, Lena stood in front of the mirror and brushed her hair. None of what had happened to her in the past few weeks made any sense at all. Her life had been turned upside down. She'd have the wedding dream tonight, she just knew it. Every time things went nutty she had the damn dream. Tossing her hairbrush to the countertop, she muttered an expletive and got in bed.

In less than ten minutes, she was marching down the aisle.

ANDRES HAD BEEN shot before, but the bullet that ripped through his left shoulder as he walked out of his building was so unexpected, so unbelievably startling, he simply didn't understand what had actually happened.

Gasping, then reeling backward, he dropped his briefcase and crashed into the wall behind him. The pain was instantaneous, a hot, black wave that exploded in his body and threatened to overwhelm him. He slid down the stucco before he could stop himself, a red trail marking his progress as his shirt snagged the roughened texture of the wall.

His breath rasping, his mind spinning, he was still for only a second. Immediately his old training kicked in, and he scrambled sideways to get behind a nearby planter. He had no idea where the shooter was, but he wanted his .38 in his hand. The lightweight pistol, in a leather leg holster, was only an inch from his fingertips, but it felt as if it were a mile. Crying out with the pain, he bent until his fingers wrapped around the cold wooden grip, the unexpected scent of pine mulch from the nearby planter reaching him as he yanked out the weapon.

The revolver was a five-shot Smith & Wesson he'd bought off an ex-CIA man, but before Andres could even think about where to aim, a second report rang out over his head. He sprang to his left with an agonizing lurch, the gun in his hand no match for the high-speed, long-distance rifle being used against him. He half ran, half stumbled toward a low wall that fronted the building itself. It'd give more cover than the planter...but not much. Just as he reached the three-foot ledge, the sniper shot once more. Whoever he was, he had a helluva aim and a damn good weapon.

But still he missed.

The window behind Andres exploded and the taste of fear filled his mouth. A second earlier, and it would have been his head instead of the glass. His shoulder screaming with pain, Andres turned, thinking he could retreat now, back inside the building through the broken window. The shot had gone high, and he saw the glass had come from a section too far above him to be reached.

There was no way he could get back inside, and no way he could get to his car.

He was trapped.

COMING UP from the nightmare was like swimming to the top of an endlessly deep pool, but the ringing phone insisted she make the journey. Groggily, Lena reached for the portable receiver with one hand and the clock with the other. It was 2:00 a.m. She'd only been asleep for a couple of hours.

"We've got a problem."

Bradley's deep voice boomed from the other end of the line, and all thought of sleep fled. Lena was fully awake before he finished speaking. "What's up?"

"We just got a report of a sniper at an office building off Highway 98."

"A sniper?" She waited for more information, but Bradley stayed silent. Was she missing something? "I don't understand. Are you saying some idiot with a gun is taking potshots at civilians for no reason? At 2:00 a.m.?"

"Something like that."

"How'd the call come in?"

"We don't have all the details yet. I think someone driving by saw something. Dispatch sent a black and white then a second-shots-fired call came in from the same location and they decided a regular unit would just be another target. They sent the run to us."

Cradling the phone between her shoulder and ear, Lena jumped out of the bed and grabbed the pants and shirt she always kept nearby. Stripping off her nightgown, she pulled on her clothes. "What's left to know? Get Alpha Team out there right now. Call Diego, too. It's probably useless, but he might be able to do something."

Without missing a beat, she juggled the receiver to her other ear and reached for her boots. "Get Sarah working on the neighborhood, too, and see if she can get something on the area. What's the address?" She snatched up her SWAT jacket and was heading toward her entry when she realized Bradley hadn't answered.

"Brad? Are you there? I'm going out the door...."

He was the calmest man Lena knew. He was the person she'd want beside her in any kind of situation. He never got rattled. When he finally spoke, she stopped. Because all at once he sounded upset.

"Well, that's the problem, Lena. That's why I'm calling...."

She was at her front door, one hand on the phone, the other on the doorknob. Later she marveled at how composed she sounded. Her voice was as smooth and flat as ice but just as thin, her heart suddenly beating inside her chest so hard it hurt. "What is it?"

"The office where this is happening...well, it's Andres's office, Lena."

Her lungs went tight and she suddenly couldn't catch her breath. "Have you tried to reach him?"

"We called his office *and* sent a unit to his condo. No one answers at either place."

"Have you located his vehicle?"

"Sarah did that first thing." She heard Bradley swallow. "His Suburban's in the parking lot...at the office."

They spoke a few more minutes, then Lena hung up the phone. She told herself to stay calm, to stay focused.

The advice went unheeded.

Two seconds later, she flew down her driveway on two screaming tires, the left side of her truck hanging in the air as she careened around the corner. She felt the jolt as the tires hit the highway's pavement and dug in, but she gunned the engine, driving through the darkness half-blind with fear.

Accusations shrieked through her head. She *should* have insisted Andres have a guard all this time. She *should* have made sure no one got close to him. She *should* never have let him out of her sight.

This was all her fault.

The road was a blur as she hurtled through the night.

HIDDEN BEHIND the wall, Andres crouched down as far as he could. He had no idea where the shooter was located, but with the right angle, he might easily be able to aim over the short brick enclosure. Andres held no illusion of safety. He couldn't depend on the P.D., either. He thought he'd seen a black and white at one point, but they'd disappeared and rightly so. They would have been pinned if they stayed. He could only pray SWAT had been called. For the moment, though, he was on his own.

With his shoulder on fire and bleeding, he turned to assess his location.

The enclosure was small. No more than six or seven feet in circumference. To the left of the front door was a mirror image of where he hid. Every morning and afternoon, the building's smokers huddled here. There was room for about five people, but from the butts on the ground, it seemed as if a legion of them came out to smoke. Over the coppery smell of his blood, Andres caught the stale scent of tobacco. It reminded him of the last time he'd smoked. When Lena had been shot.

He held his breath, then chanced a look over the wall. The mental snapshot burned into his brain as he fell back down behind his cover. There were countless places a sniper could hide: a tall apartment building directly across the street, a corner grocery to the right, a closed flower shop on the left. He suspected the apartment, though. It afforded the best view.

But it was his own parking lot that gave him the most pause. There were three vehicles in it, besides the black Suburban. Andres closed his eyes and positioned the vehicles in his mind. His SUV in the front, to the left. A red Firebird to the right. A green Jeep in the back.

And a silver Town Car by the curb across the street.

As if spurred on by the realization and not his sudden movement, blood began to pour from his wound. Andres cursed roundly into the darkness and clamped a hand over the wound. It was hell to be right after all this time.

He only hoped the truth wouldn't die with him.

LENA KEPT a steady conversation going with Bradley as she sped toward the scene, giving him instructions and getting minute-by-minute updates. The War Wagon was dispatched with record speed and set up two blocks away from Andres's office. She drove straight to the site, dropping her cell phone and the link to Bradley only when she had the team in view. Slamming the truck to a stop, she parked with two wheels on the curb and two in the street, then jumped out and sprinted toward the gathered team members. Bradley noted her entrance then turned back to the men to help distribute the gear. As she reached them, Beck came to her side.

"What have we got?" She reached for the headset he handed her and tried to keep her anxiousness from her voice. "Any news?"

Beck's eyes met hers in the darkness. "Nothing so far. Sarah's inside still trying to find Andres. She's running the tags on all the cars parked for two blocks around here, and she's contacting the other tenants who have offices in the building. We were waiting for you before we deployed.''

She turned to the nearest man. It was Brandon. ''Get me a jacket and a helmet,'' she instructed. ''I want night vision goggles, too.''

Beck put his hand out at once and stopped Brandon. ''Lena, you can't do this,'' he said sternly. ''You need to stay in the Wagon. You haven't recovered fully.''

''I'm fine.'' Her demeanor was even and so was her voice as she glanced back toward the younger cop. ''Go get the gear.''

He started off again but once more Beck stopped him, this time with a growl. ''Just a minute—''

Brandon halted his progress, but he looked askance at Lena. She *was* the commander.

''Stand down, Brandon,'' she said. ''Lieutenant Winters and I need to talk.'' The younger cop took two steps backward and locked his hands behind his back. His gaze was in the distance but his ears were almost twitching.

No one ever contradicted Lena.

''What in the hell do you think you're doing, Beck?'' she asked softly.

''I'm trying to save your butt,'' he answered. ''You aren't ready for this and even if you were, that could be Andres caught up there. You can't think straight when he's involved.''

''That's not true. And I'm fine.''

''No, you're not,'' he said, each word deliberate.

"You're upset, you're shaking, and you're going to make decisions you shouldn't if you command this operation."

She glared at Beck in the darkness and remembered Brandon's near miss all those weeks ago. Beck had a point, but suddenly she knew she'd handle this situation just as she had the last one, and would the next one and still the one after that.

She was a cop.

She had to put aside her personal life and all that entailed because lives depended on her ability to do so. She'd accepted that principle when she signed on, but she hadn't understood exactly what it meant until this very moment.

Now she did.

The awful clarity was overpowering and far-reaching. Suddenly, she understood the terrible dilemma Andres had faced when he'd gone to rescue his friend. Everything he was, everything he stood for, had come to a head with that call. He couldn't have done anything but try to save his friend, then afterward deal with the man responsible *and* the backlash. She would have done the same, even knowing her own father could have been involved.

She turned to the young cop behind her. "Get that gear and make it fast." He fled immediately then she looked up at Beck. "I'm a cop," she said quietly. "I'll make the decisions I have to and worry about the consequences later. Nothing is more important than that."

Beck's eyes held stony judgment. They were friends but she was also his boss and until this moment that relationship had never been tested. He read something in her gaze, however, something Lena suspected hadn't been there before. He nodded once, then turned away.

SILENCE ECHOED in the empty streets.

Andres was getting weaker by the moment and he had to do something fast. A plan formed in his mind as he gripped his gun and turned to stare at the window behind him. He hand-packed his own ammo, and it was powerful. One shot might be enough to shatter the thick, tempered glass. He could hit a lower pane, then crawl inside and escape through the back of the building. He'd be exposed while leaping inside but that was better than sitting here and bleeding to death. There was someone out there trying to kill him and he had to find out who.

He didn't give himself time to think about it. Andres popped up then immediately dropped and rolled to his right. Just as he wanted, the sniper responded a heartbeat later. He was a good shooter but not experienced enough to recognize the ploy. Lifting his pistol with his good hand, Andres fired quickly into the glass. The window shattered and he crawled through.

He found the nearest hall and ran toward the rear, the closed doors of all the offices silent witnesses to his flight. Stumbling blindly, he finally spotted a dim red light signaling an exit. He increased his speed and hit the door with one shoulder to sprint outside. Turning right at the corner of the building, he doubled back and disappeared into the darkness. Two seconds later he was across the street and where he needed to be.

GEARED UP and ready to go, Lena studied the map someone had thrust before her. She thought for a bit and discussed the situation with Bradley, then together they decided on a plan. They explained the deployment to the men who asked few questions; they trusted her with everything, including their lives. After a second communications check, she raised her hand and sent them out. They jogged silently down the two blocks toward the office building and within ten minutes, everyone was in place.

From her position, Lena lifted her night vision glasses and peered through the lens to the building beyond. It sprang into focus and what she witnessed made her tremble.

The ground in front of the building was littered with glass. The team's spotter had reported more shots fired just before the men had gone out. There was no sign of anyone at the moment, but someone *had* been there. He'd left a trail of blood. Her hands shook as she swept her gaze from left to right. He'd clearly been hit coming around the building and had fallen backward. She could see where he'd crashed against the wall and then slid down, a solid patch of red splattered against the stucco, just about shoulder height.

Dropping the binoculars, Lena pulled her microphone toward her mouth. "Call for an ambulance, Sarah. I think we're going to need one."

Sarah replied immediately. "Ten-four. I'll get one on the way."

She didn't want to look any more, but she had to. With even shakier hands, Lena raised the glasses once again and picked up the trail.

More blood was smeared across the sidewalk, and she followed the horrible streaks until they disappeared behind the low wall that fronted the building.

Was he still there, lying behind the wall, suffering?

Or had he already died?

CHAPTER SIXTEEN

As soon as Andres entered the apartment's garage, he remembered the building was empty. It was under renovation and he'd seen the trucks coming and going without even thinking about what that meant.

It was the perfect place for the shooter to hide; Andres would have picked it himself. The third or fourth floor, he'd estimated earlier. Good angle, quick getaway, a corner unit to see as much as possible. The whole setup felt right, and his intuition had yet to let him down.

He studied the empty garage, his shoulder going numb, black dots swimming in front of his vision. If he'd had any sense at all he would have holed up inside the office and called for backup, but he hadn't wanted to waste the time, and more importantly, he wasn't going to risk anyone else's life.

The thought renewed his energy, and Andres forced himself to press forward.

Lena wanted to scream but she spoke quietly into her microphone, calling out the code names for Cal Hamilton and Jason Field, the rear entry men. She couldn't risk approaching the offices from the front, and everyone knew why. They'd seen the blood, too. "Are you guys in place? At the back door?"

Both men answered in the affirmative. Before Lena had even gotten on-site, thanks to Sarah's hard work, the team had floor plans of Andres's building from the city inspector. They hadn't been able to find the manager, though. They had no keys.

"How's it look?" Lena asked anxiously.

Cal spoke for both of them. "Seems clear at this point. The back door's pretty protected. I think we can work our way up there and slip inside."

"Go ahead," Lena instructed, "but keep me informed."

She pressed her mike closer and spoke again. "R1, this is L1. Come in, please."

A calm, collected man whom Lena considered one of the best on the team, Ryan replied immediately. "This is R1."

"Any idea where the shooter might be?"

"Negative for now. All we know is what's most obvious—he has to be in front. If he shoots again, I might be able to triangulate his position and give you some idea, but anything else at this point would be a guess. I wasn't in place when he last fired."

"Go ahead and guess." Her mouth was almost

too dry to form the words. "It'd be better than nothing right now, and nothing is all we've got so far."

"Give me a second. I need a better angle myself."

She waited in the tension-filled silence. Because she knew where each man now was, Lena imagined that she could see them. One behind the stand of palms near the left side of the building. One crouched behind a hedge that lined the western side. One in the parking lot. She was fooling herself, though, and she knew it. With their camouflaged faces and black clothing from top to bottom, no one could be spotted without infrared gear. They had come across bad guys with that kind of equipment, but something told her this one didn't have it. He would have already been shooting if he did.

Ryan Lukas broke into her thoughts. "There's a building across the street," he said. "It's an apartment. Have Sarah call the management and see if there are any empty ones facing the offices."

Before he finished speaking, Lena relayed the message. She then checked in with the rest of the men. Each one answered quietly, but there was tension in their tones. A fellow cop was in trouble and they didn't like that.

Lena settled in to wait.

And to pray.

ANDRES MADE HIS WAY to the rear entrance of the apartment building, stepping over construction trash and trying to stay quiet. There was only one door. The lock had been jimmied, and the door itself was propped open with a chopped-off brick.

Easing past the opening, he stood quietly for a second and let his eyes adjust. The entry was cave-like; for a moment he could see nothing at all, then a darker square slowly took form to his right. It was another door, this one wide-open. He edged toward it and stepped inside, the stygian blackness claustrophobic. After a second, he realized he was in the stairwell, just as he'd hoped. With nothing but his feet to guide him, he began to go up.

The only sound he heard was his own harsh breathing and his pulse as it rushed through his body. His left arm and shoulder had no feeling at all now, and that whole side of his body was use-less, a weight that was only slowing him down. He clutched the .38 in his right hand and thanked God he'd been hit on the left side.

Panting with the effort, he made it to the third floor. A quick survey and he knew it was empty. The fourth floor was the same. He was beginning to get worried by the time he reached the fifth floor. But the door from the stairwell to the hall-way was propped open just like the one downstairs had been. Andres slipped into the deserted corri-dor. There were four doors between where he stood and the unit at the end. Each was painted a dark blue with brass numbers decorating the front. Each was closed, except the last. Gliding down the passage, he made his way to the end where he stood before the final doorway.

If he'd still been a cop, Andres would have called out, then knocked on the door, but he wasn't bound by those laws. The only thing that mattered now was Lena. He prayed she'd understand. He lifted his leg and kicked in the flimsy wooden barrier.

The man at the window rose in shock, his face revealed by the street lamp outside. Confused and incredulous, he jerked up his rifle to shoot, but Andres was faster.

With one last ounce of effort, he raised his weapon then aimed and fired. The man before him pitched to the floor, and a heartbeat later, Andres crumpled as well.

"THE APARTMENTS are empty." Sarah's voice sounded in Lena's ear. "They're being remodeled, and all the renters were kicked out about three months ago. The manager says he can—"

"*Quiet!*" Lena silenced Sarah with the command and at the same time ripped off her headset. She'd heard something while Sarah was speaking. Something that sounded like gunfire.

She strained to listen in the darkness, her pulse pounding so loudly it was impossible to hear more.

The headset in her hand began to squeak and she quickly put it back on. Beck spoke this time.

"I heard it, too," he said. He had stayed with the Wagon to coordinate. "That was gunfire."

"Check in," Lena ordered. "Who's out there? What's going on?"

One by one the men responded. No one had fired his weapon. Ryan spoke when they finished. "I think it came from the apartment, Lena. I saw a flash."

She whirled and faced the building behind her. The windows were black and unnerving; they stared back at her with blank resistance. Grabbing her mike, she spoke curtly. "Scott, you and Hamilton get over there. Check out each entrance then call in."

"Ten-four."

Two shadows detached themselves from the darkness then disappeared again. Lena only saw them because she'd placed them herself. She had no idea where they were now or which direction they'd taken; they'd be in place before anyone else would know where, either.

In the waiting silence, she refused to think about Andres or what was happening.

An endless minute passed, then two more. Scott Brody's voice finally sounded. "The front door's secure. There's a chain linked through the handles. No one could get in or out that way. The back has been propped open, though." He said something in a muffled voice about a flashlight, then he spoke again. "Linc says there are two sets of prints in the dust. Two people have gone up there, and I'd say they're still there, unless they came down a different way."

Lena measured her breathing. In and out. In and out. "What do the prints look like?" she asked calmly.

"I'm no expert," Scott said, "but one set looks like hunting boots to me. About a size eleven maybe? I'm not sure about the others. They're smooth with a heel. The same size, I'd say."

"Do you see anything else?"

"There's blood," he said. "And lots of it. It's fresh."

He continued to speak, but Lena heard nothing more. A sudden buzzing in her ears blocked all her hearing. She brought herself under control, but it wasn't an easy task.

"Can you follow it?" she asked thickly. "The blood..."

"Oh, yeah." The cop's voice was matter-of-fact. "I'd say probably we won't have to go too far, either—he's losing too much of it to keep going for long."

Lena grabbed her microphone as if it could steady her. "Cal, you and Jason get across the street. Back them up."

"What about us?" Scott asked. "You want us to go up or wait?"

"Hold your position," Lena ordered. "I'm on my way."

THEY WERE HUDDLED at the doorway, waiting. Lena alerted the four men before she made her approach, then she darted to where they were poised. They explained the layout of the building and waited for her to tell them what to do.

It didn't take long for her to assess the situation. There was only one way they *could* do it.

She looked at the blood, a chill settling in her heart, then she lifted her gaze to the expectant men. "Okay, we'll do this in twos." She nodded at Scott Brody, on her right, the cop who'd been her backup the day Andres had flown in and she'd been wounded. "Scott and Linc go first. I'll go next, then Cal and Jason follow. That way we'll have coverage front and back."

The strategy was one they'd practiced a thousand times. They nodded as she continued.

"We'll stop on each floor and do a quick sweep, but for God's sake, stay alert. Obviously we're dealing with someone who knows his way around a gun."

All four men acknowledged her warning with serious looks, then they turned toward the stairs, Scott and Linc, the two more seasoned vets, leading the silent team into the kind of hell they knew best—the unknown and the deadly. The dark couldn't have been more thick, and Lena's heart couldn't have beaten any faster.

On the fifth floor they found them both. One dead, one alive.

One her lover, one her brother.

CHAPTER SEVENTEEN

ANDRES KNEW when they found him.

He felt Lena's hands on his chest—her sweet, soft hands—ripping off his shirt, her nails raking over his skin, her touch brutish as she tried desperately to get to his wound. He opened his eyes as cold air brushed against his bare skin. He couldn't move his left arm, and his right felt as though it were tied to the floor. Despite this, he tried to wave her off.

She captured his fingers with hers, and in an eerie echo of him, she said, "No…no, Andres. Don't move—be still! The medics are on the way."

"God, Lena…what are you doing here? Go…go away." He struggled to get the words out. "Please, please don't…don't look—"

She spoke as if he'd said nothing, and then he wondered if he had gotten the warning out or simply imagined giving it voice.

"He's dead." Her voice cracked. "Wh-what happened, Andres? What in the hell just happened here?"

"J-Jeff was the one behind everything, Lena." With each word, Andres felt more blood leak from his shoulder, but he had to speak. The pain in Lena's voice was much worse than what was happening to him. "He was the one sending money to the Red Tide. N-not your father."

He felt his sight ebbing, a darkness intruding on the edge of his vision. He was going into shock, his blood pressure dropping. "I'm sorry, Lena...I didn't figure it out until tonight.... I read Carmen's notes and saw Jeff had defended Escada. I-I was coming to tell you. He knew I was close.... He had to stop me himself. He—he couldn't risk another miss...."

Lena bent over him, and he smelled the scent of her skin. It seemed strange, lying in the dirt and the blood, to catch that hint of sweetness.

"Oh, God, Andres..." Her voice broke completely. He could hear her stop and draw a breath of her own. It was ragged and filled with agony. "Oh, God...this is all my fault! I should have known. When you told me about Dad, I confronted him, and he acted so strange. I could tell something was going on, but I didn't understand. He must have guessed! He suspected Jeff all along, and he was protecting him...."

Through the growing murk of his vision, Andres summoned his last bit of strength to look at Lena. She was holding a flashlight, the beam weak and unsteady but strong enough to reveal her face. She was covered with camouflage makeup, dark-green streaks mixed with black. Her T-shirt was torn on one sleeve and her gorgeous hair was matted to her head. She'd never looked more beautiful or been more precious.

He'd love her forever.

STANDING IN the center of her brother's tiny apartment, Lena looked around her, nothing but dead silence and dusty air keeping her company. After many hours of work, the forensic team had left. The investigators had departed shortly after that. She'd wanted to stay at the hospital but the doctors had told her there was nothing she could do, so she'd left Andres in their hands. She'd arrived in time to get a quick report from the lead man, a report she now wished she hadn't heard.

How could she have been so blind? How could she have missed what Jeff had become?

With grief and disappointment weighing her down, she walked slowly across the living room and stood in the doorway of her brother's bedroom. He'd pushed the bed against one wall and lined the rest of the room with cheap metal tables. Their surfaces were covered with a jumbled mess of books, writing tablets and various magazines. The investigators had boxed up and taken out over a dozen different notebooks. One quick glance at their pages had told them everything: Jeff's long-standing connection to the Red Tide. His idealism taken to madness...his excruciating need to prove something to Phillip that even he couldn't articulate. He'd filled hundreds of spiral-bound pages with every detail.

Tacked to the drywall above the tables were photographs. The investigators had left them after videotaping the room. Their content made no sense—there were movie stars, pages from war books, even drawings Jeff had done himself. One in particular caught Lena's eye. She crossed the room and took out the pin holding it to the wall.

It was a pen-and-ink sketch. The details weren't perfect, but she had no trouble recognizing herself and Jeff. He'd drawn them—as children—on the beach right outside her home. They couldn't have been more than seven and five. She sat down heavily on his bed, the paper crackling between her fingers.

Why? Why had he done this?

Hot, stinging tears filled her eyes and overflowed, but no answer came with them. It seemed impossible that Jeff had been able to live a double life with no one being aware of it, but obviously he had. It'd started with Pablo Escada's trial. He'd handled it for the firm, his notes full of excitement at the possibility of doing something "worthwhile." Lena had stared in disbelief as the investigator had shown her that passage. Escada had recruited Jeff with talk of a revolution and a better life for the poor of the islands. And Jeff had fallen for it completely.

She looked at the drawing in her hands, but didn't really see it, her breaking heart filled with sorrow. Convincing Jeff to join the Red Tide would have been an easy task for Escada. Jeff had always been the one on the outside, the one who didn't fit in. He hadn't known what he was really getting into, though. The little boy who'd chased her into the waves then warned her about the monsters had found them himself.

Feeling older than she was, Lena pushed herself up from the bed and went to the small closet in one corner of the room. Someone had left the light on inside. Reaching around the corner to the switch, something caught her eye on the floor. When she bent down, she realized it was one of Jeff's notebooks. Dropped or simply missed, it'd been left behind.

She stood there for a moment and trembled. The little bit she'd been shown had been painful enough; could she stand any more?

But she did what she had to and opened the cover. The hate-filled message jumped out at her, the vitriolic words scribbled so hard the ink had gone through to the next page. She skimmed the first page and went on to the next. She read until the writing was blurred by new tears.

Jeff had hated Phillip beyond all reason. He'd

done everything he could to make Phillip look guilty, while trying to keep Lena safe.

She lifted her eyes and blinked, remembering his attempt to save her. He'd told her to marry Andres and move to Miami and have babies. In his tangled confusion, he'd wanted her away from everything, and possibly Andres as well. The notes trembled in her hand and a tear fell to the opened page, smearing the ink.

"I can't handle another screwup like the last one," he wrote. "I'll have to do the job myself. I like Andres but I can't risk hurting Lena again, and she'll show up. She loves him too much not to be there. I'll have to take care of this myself. He can't stand in the way of what I have to do. Eventually she'll forgive me."

She closed the notebook and a sob caught in her throat. Of course she would forgive him. He'd been her brother and always would be. She had loved him; they'd shared more than just a mother and father.

She'd forgive him, but she'd never understand.

ON THE PATIO OF Phillip's home a week later—a lifetime later—Lena stood with her back to the door and the crowd that had gathered. She was still numb, numb and angry, a paralyzing grief too breathtaking to even describe filling her heart and mind. They knew no more now than they had the first day, but she'd read more of Jeff's diaries. With each word, she'd felt worse.

She tried to shut out the noise behind her, but she couldn't. The crowd was too big, the sound of their chatter too deafening. None of these people had really known her brother, she told herself. A second later she realized the irony of that thought. She hadn't known him, either.

Wrapping her arms around herself and shivering in the cool winter breeze, she stared out over the lawn.

The worst part had been telling Phillip. She'd tried to make it as easy for him as she could. She'd actually lifted the notebook she'd found—even though it was technically evidence—and stashed it at her house. Later, if necessary, she could "find" it and turn it in. Why did her father need to know how much Jeff had hated him? How he'd done everything in his power to set Phillip up and make him look guilty?

As if her thoughts had conjured him, Lena heard footsteps behind her. She turned to find her father walking toward her. He looked even more frail than he had before, and she wondered if he could survive this.

Without saying a word, he came to her side and put his arm around her. They stood quietly, each lost in thought, then he spoke.

"I'm sorry, Lena. I'm so sorry all this happened. I've been the worst father in the world."

"That's not true, Dad." Lena turned and met Phillip's watery blue gaze. "You did what you thought was best."

"I never thought Jeff would actually try to hurt anyone or I would have—"

"You weren't sure. You didn't have proof. What could you have done?"

"At the very least, I should have told you my suspicions. You're such a good cop, I guess I thought you were invincible.... I just assumed you could always take care of yourself, no matter what."

Lena couldn't believe her ears. Her father had actually said she was a *good* cop?

"But I'm a blind old man and a foolish one, too. Just after you were shot, Bering and I discovered money was missing from the firm. He knew Jeff had handled the Escada case and began to put it together. When you came looking for me, he called me in Atlanta and told me because we were afraid you might find out we'd been investigating Jeff. I had gone there to talk to another lawyer, a woman who'd done some work for Escada."

Lena remembered Bering's startled look when she'd asked him about Pablo Escada, his reluctance to talk to her that day. It made sense now.

Phillip gripped the railing of the balcony. His hands were spotted, the veins large under the papery skin. "I even put an investigator on the case. We were doing all we could but Jeff didn't give us enough time. I couldn't accuse him without being sure.''

He looked toward the pool, his eyes unfocused.

''Jeff was the only one who seemed to care. He did the pro bono work and handled the cases no one else would. We gave him a hard time for what he did. I didn't understand....''

''None of us did, Dad. Don't beat yourself up over it. You were trying. We just didn't know who he was.''

Footsteps sounded on the patio behind them, and in unison, they turned. Andres walked slowly toward them, his left arm bound against his chest, his black hair gleaming in the weak winter sun. He'd only gotten out of the hospital the day before and they hadn't had a real chance to talk since everything had happened. There had been too much confusion and too many details to handle.

Lena wondered now if they hadn't talked because they didn't know what to say to each other. He was pale beneath his tan and there were shadows behind his eyes, but his ever present aura of sensuality and power radiated toward her as persistently as it ever had, maybe even more so. Her heart jumped inside her chest and begin to knock painfully against her ribs.

Phillip spoke first. ''Hello, Andres.''

Andres appeared to pull his eyes from Lena's face with an almost physical effort. He turned to Phillip and nodded, but he didn't say a word.

Phillip stared straight back. Lena could feel the tension between the two of them just as she had before, but now—at last—she understood. Phillip had suspected all along that Andres was getting closer and closer to the real culprit behind the Red Tide. He'd been afraid for his son.

Her father spoke abruptly, spitting out the words as though he wanted to get them out before he could change his mind. "I owe you an apology, Andres. If I hadn't been so stubborn, there are people who might be alive instead of dead. I don't know what to say except I was wrong, and you were right. I'm sorry for everything that happened, although I understand that's no excuse."

Lena watched as Andres shook his head, one thick lock of his black hair falling over his forehead. She was sure her father didn't see what she did; the way Andres's eyes changed and filled with pity.

"You don't owe me an apology, Phillip. I'm the one who should offer the apology. My suspicions of you were unfounded. I'm sorry for suspecting you. The truth is Jeff would have done whatever he wanted to, regardless of what you did. He was past the point of logic."

"My son just tried to kill you. He had your best friend and your assistant murdered. He almost killed Lena. Are you telling me you can forgive him all that? I'm not sure I can...."

Lena reached out and put her hand on her father's arm. His voice was agonized.

"It's not my job to forgive anyone," Andres replied quietly. "But I understand the situation. Jeff wasn't thinking straight. If he had been, he would never have done any of those things. That's all I can really say."

"I don't understand," Phillip said, shaking his head. "I just don't understand."

"Jeff didn't think there was any other way," Andres answered. "He *had* to have Carmen silenced. She was getting too close, just as I was. As for Mateo, I don't think Jeff even knew I was involved at that point. He was sending the Red Tide money and that was all. They found out about Mateo somehow and used Jeff's money to bribe the right people and have him killed. It had nothing to do with me. Nothing at all...."

They spoke a bit more, then finally, a few minutes later, Phillip left to tend to his guests. Andres moved closer to where Lena stood. He smelled like soap and fresh air. She couldn't resist lifting a hand to place it on his cheek. "How do you feel?"

He put his fingers over hers and squeezed gently before taking his hand away. "I think I'll be all right."

"You think?" Andres wasn't a man who used qualifiers.

"It all depends," he said.

"On what?"

"On you."

She stayed silent. She didn't know what to say.

"I left you at the altar. I accused your father of being a criminal. Now this…I don't know where to begin to heal the hurts between us, Lena. I don't know if you can forgive me."

"I love you," she said softly. "There's nothing between us that time can't handle…and nothing to forgive."

His gaze was black and unfathomable. "You told me before you couldn't trust me, that you weren't sure I wouldn't leave you again. Do you still feel that way?"

Her throat ached with the effort of answering him. She wasn't sure she could explain herself. "Oh, Andres… When I was outside the office building—when I realized that you'd been hit—something happened inside me. All I can say is that suddenly I understood why you did what you did, and the truth is I would have done the very same thing."

"But Jeff—"

She stopped him. "Andres, you didn't have a choice. And I understand that completely—I'm a cop. I'll miss my brother the rest of my life and there's…" she faltered, her voice turning thick before she could control herself and start over. "There's always going to be a hole in my heart where I loved him. But the man you had to shoot wasn't the person I knew. He wasn't my little brother. That hurts so deeply I can't even explain it. He was my brother, but he was a stranger.''

She blinked the tears back, her eyes filling anyway. ''You're aren't like that. You're exactly who you say you are. And you live the principles that mean so much to us both. You're going to be the one who gets me through this, Andres. I couldn't do it without you.''

''Are you sure?''

''Absolutely. If you hadn't done what you did, I wouldn't love you. And that's what it all boils down to. I love you and I always will. I know that with my brain *and* with my heart. For once, they're in total agreement.''

She expected him to say something, something that would make everything all right between them once more, but he managed to surprise her even so.

He reached out and cupped her cheek with his free hand. ''Does this mean you'll marry me?''

Without saying a word, she put her arms around him and pressed herself against his chest with care. She could feel his heart beating between them—or maybe it was her own.

He responded by bending his head and kissing her deeply. When they broke apart a few moments later, she looked into his eyes and answered him once and for all, full of the knowledge that she was doing the right thing.

"There's nothing I'd like better than to be your wife, Andres." Her voice broke as she uttered the words, and then her tears flowed freely. She spoke past the ache in her throat, past the stinging release. "I'd be honored to be your wife. Now and forever."

He nodded with satisfaction and drew her close once more. As the sea breeze blew through the palms, they kissed again and dreamed of their future together.

EPILOGUE

LENA MCKINNEY stepped onto the red-carpeted aisle of the flower-filled church, the solemn strains of the "Wedding March" drifting above the crowded pews.

All the guests were watching her and she knew what they were thinking—Lena McKinney was *finally* getting married. Her single years were behind her, and now she was with the man she loved. From beneath her lacy veil she smiled with silent satisfaction, then all at once, the realization hit her.

It really was happening! They were actually getting married!

Andres smiled and held out his hand and Lena walked toward him to take his fingers in hers.

His warm grip was as real as the rest of the moment. Ten minutes later they were husband and wife.

What happens when two high-profile
members of a SWAT team clash?
Find out in Kay David's

THE LISTENER

Coming in May 2001
(Harlequin Superromance 985)

Now turn the page for
an exciting preview.

CHAPTER ONE

"Do you enjoy ruining people's lives or is it just me you have it in for?"

As he towered over her desk, Ryan Lukas's wrath was so intense, so powerful, it filled Maria Worley's office with an almost physical presence. She was accustomed to handling angry men, but *his* fury was different. Above a clenched jaw and an angry mouth, the black ice of his eyes revealed a storm just waiting to be unleashed.

At her.

She spoke quietly, calmly. "Is that what you think I'm doing?"

At her question, his expression turned fractionally darker and his mouth, already a violent slash, narrowed into a line of disbelief. He was so tightly wound the changes were subtle, but Maria was an expert at reading faces. It was her job. For the past three years she'd been the chief psychologist for the Emerald Coast SWAT team. The cops who were her clients were all men on the edge, trapped between the realities they faced and the way the rest of the world worked. Men who didn't know what to do with themselves or the disasters they'd become. Men who didn't know where to turn.

Men like Ryan Lukas.

"If you put me on some kind of bogus leave, that's exactly what you'll be doing!" He glared at her, an imposing column of churning emotion. "I want to work and I *should* be working. The team needs me. Besides that, there's nothing wrong with me."

"If that's really the case, then you'll be back on active duty in record time. Until then, because of the tests we did last week during your routine assessment and the talks we've had so far, I feel the need for further evaluation of your situation. As soon as I'm comfortable with your progress, I'll release you."

"And Lena agrees with this bullsh—"

Lena McKinney was Ryan Lukas's boss and commander of the SWAT team. Maria didn't envy her the job. "Lieutenant McKinney and I have discussed the matter, yes. She believes, as I do, that you need some time off. That's why she moved up your yearly evaluation. She was concerned about you and wanted me to assess you before things got out of hand. Taking everything into consideration, Lieutenant Lukas, surely you can understand—"

"I understand one thing," he said icily. "I understand that you're screwing with me...and I'm going to pay the price. One way or another."

Maria looked out her window and tried to gather

her thoughts. The office faced the Gulf of Mexico, and in the distance, the sparkling water glinted like diamonds. Generally she didn't argue with her patients, but Ryan Lukas wasn't like most of her clients. She faced him once more.

"Lieutenant Lukas, anyone who has faced what you have needs to talk about it. Anyone. If you don't believe me, look at the problems you've experienced lately. Emotions escape any way they can, even when it means causing more trouble. Don't you think you need to deal with these feelings in a more productive way?"

"I am dealing with them." His eyes locked on hers. "My way."

She waited for him to elaborate but he wasn't going to—it was his way of taking control. During his initial visit, he'd sat without saying a word for more than half the session. It was the first time she'd had to break a client's silence. She'd never been outwaited before.

"Well, your way isn't working. Ignoring your emotions is not a good way of dealing with them." She paused a moment. "And don't try to convince me you have no feelings about the situation. That's impossible."

At his side, his hands clamped into fists. She wondered if he was conscious of the movement.

"I never said I had no feelings about what happened." He stopped for a second, then seemed to gather himself. "I do. But I don't intend to share them with you or anyone else."

"Even if it means your job?"

"My wife's…situation had nothing to do with my job."

She noted the word he used; he couldn't even say *death*. It was time to be blunt.

"That's a lie, Lieutenant, and you know that as well as I do. You're one of the most important members of the SWAT team. You have to be sharp, on your toes. What happens at home impacts your ability to think and to make decisions. Everyone understands that. Surely you do, too."

His eyes glittered, two black sapphires, dark and hard. "Do you perform marriage counseling?"

The unexpected question took her by surprise and she answered without thinking. "Of course. That's one of the primary focuses of my practice."

"Are you married?"

She saw the trap now. There was nothing to do but answer him. "No," she admitted reluctantly. "I'm divorced. But my personal situation isn't pertinent—"

"And neither is mine. I can do my job, just like you can."

"That's not a fair comparison. I don't shoot people for a living."

He waited a moment to answer her, but somehow it felt longer to Maria. When he finally did speak, his voice was deliberate, each word distinct. "And do you have a problem with what I do?"

"You're a valued member of the team and what you have to do is necessary. How I feel about your job is not important. What matters is how *you* feel about it."

"You didn't answer my question."

"It's not relevant."

"It is to me."

"And why is that?"

"I need your approval. You've already told Lena I can't do my job right now. If you have some kind of hangup with what I do—"

She interrupted him, something else she rarely did with patients, her exasperation getting the upper hand over her professionalism. "Lieutenant Lukas, I assure you my evaluation of your situation will not be influenced by your position on the team. I'm paid to look at you as an individual and that's exactly what I do. What I think about your career choice simply isn't germane to this."

"Then let me do my job."

"I can't." She made her expression flat, her voice unequivocal. "Not until we've talked more and I feel confident you've recovered from the stress of your wife's death." She pulled her calendar toward her and ran a pen down the edge of one side. Looking up, she spoke. "I have this same time open next week. I'd like to meet with you then, but if that's not convenient, you can check with my receptionist on the way out for a different time. One way or the other, I want to see you in here this coming week.'' Reaching across her desk, she put down her pen, then picked up one of her appointment cards and held it out to him, her hand in the air a full ten seconds before he finally took the offering.

Rising to his feet, he clenched the card without looking at it. ''You're making a big mistake.''

Even though he was giving her a hard time, behind his rage, his gaze was so full of pain and grief a wave of sympathy hit her. He was hurting.

''I'm sorry you see it that way,'' she said quietly. ''But I believe if we work together, I can help you.'' She rose and held out her hand for him. ''I really can.''

He ignored her outstretched fingers. ''And if I don't want your help?''

She dropped her hand. ''I'm afraid you don't have a choice, Lieutenant.''

He gave her a look that would have quailed another woman's resolve. Maria simply stared back. A second later, he pivoted sharply and stalked out. As he reached the outer hallway, she heard the sound of paper ripping. The scraps of her card fluttered gently to the carpet and then he was gone.

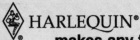

If you enjoyed what you just read,
then we've got an offer you can't resist!

Take 2 bestselling
love stories FREE!
Plus get a FREE surprise gift!

INDULGE IN A QUIET MOMENT
WITH HARLEQUIN

Get a FREE
Quiet Moments
Bath
Spa

with just two proofs of purchase from
any of our four special collector's editions in May.

**Harlequin® is sure to make your time special this Mother's Day
with four special collector's editions featuring a short story
PLUS a complete novel packaged together in one volume!**

Collection #1   Intrigue abounds in a collection featuring *New York Times*
bestselling author Barbara Delinsky and Kelsey Roberts.

Collection #2   Relationships? Weddings? Children? = *New York Times*
bestselling author Debbie Macomber and Tara Taylor Quinn
at their best!

Collection #3   Escape to the past with *New York Times* bestselling author
Heather Graham and Gayle Wilson.

Collection #4   Go West! With *New York Times* bestselling author
Joan Johnston and Vicki Lewis Thompson!

Plus Special Consumer Campaign!
Each of these four collector's editions will feature a
"FREE QUIET MOMENTS BATH SPA" offer.
See inside book in May for details.

Only from

HARLEQUIN®
Makes any time special ®

Don't miss out! Look for this exciting promotion on sale in May 2001,
at your favorite retail outlet.

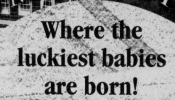

MAITLAND MATERNITY

MAITLAND MATERNITY

Where the luckiest babies are born!

In April 2001, look for

HER BEST FRIEND'S BABY
by Vicki Lewis Thompson

A car accident leaves surrogate mother Mary-Jane Potter's baby-to-be without a mother—

and causes the father, Morgan Tate, to fuss over a very pregnant Mary-Jane like a mother hen. Suddenly, Mary-Jane is dreaming of keeping the baby...and the father!

Each book tells a different story about the world-renowned Maitland Maternity Clinic— where romances are born, secrets are revealed... and bundles of joy are delivered.

HARLEQUIN®
Makes any time special ™

Silhouette®
Where love comes alive ™

Visit us at www.eHarlequin.com   MMCNM-8

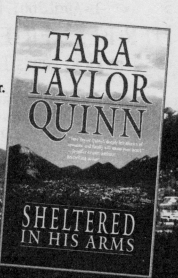